SWEET MATCHMAKING

A CANDLE BEACH SWEET ROMANCE

NICOLE ELLIS

D1491211

1

_____

"Have a nice day," Sarah Rigg called out to a woman near the exit of To Be Read. Sarah had helped her discover a new author and the woman had bought all the books in both of the author's cozy mystery series.

The woman turned and smiled, her gray hair swinging in a perfect bob around her pert chin. "You too." Then she disappeared into the sunny afternoon, the bells over the door jingling merrily as it closed.

Sarah looked around the bookstore. All of the customers were busy browsing the books and didn't appear ready to buy yet, so she left the cash register area to tidy up the store. She was busy rearranging the display of thriller novels in the bay window when Dahlia Callahan, the bookstore's owner, came out of the back room carrying a stack of books.

"How's business today?" Dahlia asked, handing a few of the books to Sarah to place in the window.

"Pretty good. A lot of tourist business. With Labor Day weekend approaching, I think most of the overnight lodging in town is fully rented."

Dahlia nodded. "Good. We need all the sales we can get. We're lucky if we get half the sales per month the rest of the year as we do in summer." She eyed Sarah. "Actually, I wanted to talk with you about that."

Sarah finished arranging the display and moved away from the bay window. "Sure. What's up?"

"So," Dahlia began, "I know we talked about you only being here for the summer, but I was hoping you'd consider working some weekends during the school year."

Sarah looked down at her feet. Did she want to work that much? Being a fourth grade teacher could be time-consuming and she wasn't sure if she could handle the extra hours. Then again, she didn't have much of a life outside of the classroom. And, it would help her earn enough money for a down payment on a house in Candle Beach if she wanted to move forward with that.

"I don't know," she said. "I love working here, but I'd need my hours to be flexible in case I have things going on at school. Can I think about it?" She hated the idea of letting Dahlia down, but she didn't want to wear herself out. She'd found that when she took on too much, she wasn't able to be as creative in the classroom or be there for her students as much.

Dahlia smiled. "Of course. I've loved having you work here too, and I don't want to lose you. You have no idea how many high schoolers I've had take the job and then bail on me two weeks later."

Sarah laughed. "I can imagine." Although she herself had always been what some may call excessively responsible, she'd had friends in high school that fit Dahlia's description.

A large family entered the bookstore, bringing with them a draft of warm ocean air. Sarah and Dahlia moved toward the espresso bar in the back, so as not to block the front door.

"I'm going to grab a cup of coffee. I'm exhausted," Dahlia said. "Do you want one?"

"A latte would be great. I've got a late night ahead of me."

"Really? What do you have planned?" Dahlia asked as she expertly tamped down coffee grounds in a metal cup and inserted it into the espresso maker. The machine hissed as boiling water hit the grounds. "Something fun I hope."

"Sorry to disappoint you, but no." Sarah surveyed the customers in the bookstore to see if anyone needed assistance. A few were browsing the shelves and a mother was reading to her small daughter in the children's section. No one looked like they needed help anytime soon, so she hopped on a stool in front of the espresso bar. "I've got that Drama in the Classroom course tomorrow at the University of Washington and I need to pack and get ready for it."

"Ooh," Dahlia's eyes lit up. "That sounds fun. I know you mentioned that you were going to attend a class there, but I didn't know what it was." She handed Sarah her drink, then dumped the used grounds in the compost bin before preparing her own coffee.

"I went last year to the entry-level class, but this is the next one in the series." Sarah sipped her latte, licking foam off of her lips before setting the cup down on the bar.

"Is anyone else from your school going?" Dahlia moved her own freshly made coffee to the side and cleaned the espresso machine with a damp cloth.

"No one from my school. There's a guy from an elementary in Haven Shores that went last year and is going this year."

Dahlia perked up. "Is he single?"

Sarah laughed. "Really? That's the first thing you ask?"

3

"Well, you're always complaining about the lack of eligible bachelors in the area." She grinned. "So, is this guy single?"

She couldn't resist teasing Dahlia. "He is for now, but I have a plan to convince him to marry me and move to Candle Beach."

Dahlia's mouth gaped open and her eyes narrowed. "You aren't serious, are you?"

"No." Sarah smiled. "Patrick's a great guy and we've loosely kept in touch since last year, but he's in a long-term relationship. He emailed me to let me know he'd be attending the class again this year though."

"Okay, so he's not a dating prospect, but can you at least carpool with him to Seattle?"

Sarah shook her head. "He's going up a day early to meet up with some friends." She'd hoped to travel with Patrick because she enjoyed being around him and she hated to drive. That plan hadn't worked out, so she planned to distract herself with audiobooks on the long trip.

"That's too bad." Dahlia swigged the rest of her coffee. "It would have been nice for you to have someone to go with. That drive can be long when you're by yourself."

"I'm okay with that." Sarah smiled, thinking about the list of audiobooks she'd been meaning to listen to but never had the time for. "I've got my eye on that Christmas romance in the audiobook section." She pointed at the small wall display of audiobooks.

Dahlia looked at where she was pointing. "Good choice. Susannah Garrity is wonderful."

"Yeah, you have to say that." When he'd first come to Candle Beach, Dahlia's now-husband Garrett had managed to keep his romance novelist alter ego private, but by now most of the town was in on the secret.

Dahlia's cheeks flushed, and she sputtered a little. "No, the reviews are good on it and I've heard the narrator is excellent."

"I was kidding." Sarah went around to the back of the bar and set her cup in the small dishwasher that had been cleverly concealed in a cabinet. "I really have been looking forward to listening to it because several customers recommended it to me just this week."

"Oh." Dahlia grinned, then said behind the back of her hand, "I sometimes worry I'll over-recommend his books to customers, just because I know the author." She peered at Sarah. "You know, if you worked here during the school year, you'd get discounts on audiobooks all year long."

Sarah mock glared at her.

Dahlia laughed and held up her hands. "I'm just saying. I know how much you love your audiobooks."

Sarah paused at the end of the bar and leaned against it, her fingers splayed across the top of the smooth, dark wood. The money would come in handy, but was buying a house by herself a silly dream? It had always been near the top of her list of life goals, but she hadn't expected to be doing it on her own.

"You look like you're lost in thought," Dahlia commented.

"I was." Sarah looked up at her. "I've been thinking lately that I'd really like to buy a house here in Candle Beach and put down my own roots. I love being back here with my family and working at the elementary. Plus, it would be nice to not have to worry about my landlord increasing my rent or wanting to sell the house I live in."

"But?" Dahlia's eyes bored into her face.

Sarah sighed. "But it's so expensive to buy a house on my own. I'd always thought I'd be married with two-point-five kids by now and living in a house with a white picket fence. It's daunting to think of doing it alone."

"Why?" Dahlia asked. "I can see the expense part of it, but you have a good job and you know this is where you want to be. I say go for it. Houses are only going to go up in price."

"Maybe." Sarah still wasn't sure, but saving money towards her future couldn't hurt. If she budgeted her time well and cut down on her guilty pleasure – watching The Bachelor and other reality shows – she would still be able to teach at the level she expected of herself and work at the bookstore too. "Anyway, I can work a few shifts a week during the school year. Maybe an evening shift twice a week and one weekend day. Would that work?"

Relief crossed Dahlia's face. "That would be amazing." She hugged Sarah. "Thank you so much. With everything going on in my life, this is one less thing to worry about."

Sarah cocked her head to the side. "Is everything okay?"

"Everything's fine," Dahlia said breezily. "Nothing to worry about." She jutted her thumb toward the back room. "I'd better get back to ordering books though. I'll be back out here in an hour to take over for you when your shift ends."

"See you." Sarah watched her friend and employer exit the public area of the bookstore. Something was bothering her, but she wasn't sure what.

"Miss," an elderly man said from behind her. "I'm ready to check out now." He had an armful of woodworking books and smelled of peppermints, reminding her of her own grandfather.

She pasted a smile on her face and took the hardcover books from his outstretched arms. "Of course. I can help you over here." She led him over to the cash register.

As soon as he left, Marsha Raines, the mayor's wife, walked in. She surveyed the store. "I just can't get over how nice it looks in here. Dahlia's done a wonderful job. Her Aunt Ruth would be so proud of her."

Sarah smiled. "I'll be sure to tell her. Can I help you find something?"

Marsha gave her the name of a mystery novel that her daughter had recommended, and Sarah helped her locate it. Marsha excitedly took the book over to one of the comfortable armchairs in the corner to flip through it. On the way back from the mystery section, Sarah snagged an empty ceramic coffee cup that someone had left on a shelf and carried it back to the espresso bar. Sometimes she wondered about the advisability of having coffee drinks available in a store full of paper books, but she did enjoy the convenience of having the coffee there herself.

When she was satisfied that the store was in good condition, she sat down on the stool behind the front desk and pulled out her phone to do some quick calculations. Grabbing a piece of paper out of the drawer beneath the counter, she jotted down a few notes. With the extra shifts at the bookstore, she would have enough for a minimal down payment on a house by December. Her heart beat faster at the thought of spending the next Christmas in her own home – one that would have room for her collection of ceramic Christmas houses and a living room with space for a freshly-cut tree. The idea was enticing.

But did she want to continue working long hours indefinitely to afford the monthly mortgage payment on her own? She shook her head. It didn't all need to be decided right now. For now, she'd earn extra money and make the decision later about becoming a homeowner.

2
_____

*P*atrick Willett raised his hand over his eyes to shield them from the late summer sun. The three-story Victorian home he'd been remodeling in one of the original residential areas of Haven Shores was taking shape. She was beautiful, with white paint, a new metal roof that could weather the torrential winter storms, and a navy-blue door. The inside wasn't quite finished, but he was hoping it might be ready to sell by next spring.

It was the third home he'd remodeled in town, and at one point he'd hoped it would be his forever home – his and Nina's. That was, until she'd left him to go "find herself" in Latin America, whatever that meant. All he knew was he wasn't a part of her life anymore.

He circled the house, admiring the neatly painted back deck and the small garden he'd put in over the summer. He'd coaxed a rosebush up the side of a white trellis and it had scented a corner of the yard with its pink flowers. A white wrought iron table and chairs sat on a patio made of large flat stones.

It was easy to imagine little kids running across the yard,

playing in the sprinkler. He'd envisioned them being his own kids, but that wasn't going to happen. The house was a perfect home for a family and he hoped that whoever purchased it would love it as much as he had.

A car's tires crackled across loose gravel as it pulled up alongside the sidewalk in front of the house. He wasn't expecting anyone. Patrick came around the side of the house and opened the white garden gate to see who had arrived.

Parker Gray stepped out of the late-model sedan and shut the door. He shaded his eyes as Patrick had done and surveyed the exterior of the house. "It looks great, Patrick."

Patrick smiled. "It's got a little bit more to go, but yeah, I think it's my best project yet."

"That's what my buyers thought." Parker loosened his striped tie and the collar of his crisply-starched white shirt. He must have come from a client meeting, because otherwise it was way too hot to wear such formal attire.

Patrick raised his eyebrows. "Your buyers? The house isn't for sale yet."

Patrick had gotten to know Parker when a client of his bought one of Patrick's houses a few years prior. They'd been friends ever since, although he saw less of Parker now that he'd moved up to Candle Beach to be closer to his fiancée, Gretchen.

"I have a couple looking for an updated historic home in the area and they've found something wrong with every house I've shown them so far. I showed them a picture of your house and they went crazy."

Huh. Patrick walked over to the porch steps and grabbed the mason jar of iced tea he'd set on the second stair, the condensation on the glass making it slick in his hands. He gulped the strong unsweetened brew and then wiped his brow with a handkerchief he pulled from his pocket.

A sharp pang ran through him at the thought of actually selling the house. It wasn't really the potential loss of the house that bothered him, but the loss of the memories that he'd hoped would be made in it. Still though, he had to give up on those kinds of thoughts. Having a buyer already interested in the house wasn't exactly a bad thing. Most people renovating a house for sale would kill for that opportunity.

He set the drink down on the step and turned back to Parker. "I'll think about it, okay?"

Parker flashed him a smile. "Sure. But if you're interested, don't wait too long. My buyers want to settle on something soon."

"Oh, but this one will be worth the wait," Patrick joked. "In all seriousness though, I'm not quite through with the renovations. It probably won't be done until early next year." Although he had his summers free, his work as a fifth grade teacher at an elementary school in Haven Shores kept him busy during the school year and he didn't anticipate progressing very quickly on the remodel once school started.

"That's okay. They're willing to wait, but if they're going to put off purchasing something until then, they want to make sure they have a contract in place."

Patrick nodded. "I understand. I'll try to let you know in the next few days." It didn't surprise him in the slightest that Parker was pursuing the house before it was on the market. He was a go-getter in the real estate world and excelled at his job.

Parker eyed Patrick. "Is it hard to part with the house with Nina gone?"

He shrugged. "Yes and no. I'm over her, but I had plans for this house. It's tough to let them go."

"Maybe starting over in a new house will be good for you – a fresh start."

"Maybe." Patrick wasn't sure about that. A new house would be much the same as the old one. There wasn't a wife or kids waiting for him in either.

"Have you heard from Nina at all?"

"No," Patrick said shortly.

"Well, maybe it was for the best. You deserve better than that."

"Ha!" Patrick laughed. "I may deserve it, but that doesn't mean the perfect woman is going to appear in my life."

"You never know. Gretchen appeared in my life when I was least expecting it."

"Uh-huh." Parker had been incredibly lucky, but that didn't mean he'd have the same good fortune. "I'll let you know about the house, okay?"

"Sounds good." Parker motioned to his car. "I was down here for the morning, but I've got to get back up to Candle Beach to show some other clients a house there. Maybe we can grab lunch next time I'm here? I'm interested to find out about any new projects you have in the works."

"Nothing yet, but I'll be looking for a new place to renovate soon. Give me a call and we can talk about lunch."

"Will do. In the meantime, I'll keep an eye out for new fixer-uppers on the market." Parker gave him a half wave, then got back into his car and drove away.

Patrick stayed outside for a while longer, then entered the house. He ran his hand over the carved wooden railing. It had taken him days to sand it down and get the stain just right, but it had been worth it. Someone, maybe Parker's client, was going to love this house. Enough lollygagging though. He had work to do. He needed to finish the subway tiles in the main bathroom's shower before he left on Sunday to see his friend near Seattle and then attend the Drama in the Classroom class he'd signed up for.

He grabbed the box of tiles and carried it into the bathroom. The space hadn't seemed so big to him before, but now he could see that tiling it would take him longer than he'd expected. However, something about working with his hands was soothing, and with the radio playing classic rock he found himself getting lost in the rhythm of his work. Soon, he'd need to set up his classroom and get back to the daily grind, but for today, he was just going to enjoy the last days of summer.

3

---

*A*t seven o'clock on Monday morning, Sarah threw her suitcase into the back of her Honda Civic and slid onto the cloth seat of the driver's side. She took a moment to compose herself and then turned the key in the ignition. Ever since she'd been in a bad car accident in her late teens, she'd hated to drive. As in hated with a passion. One of the big reasons she loved living in Candle Beach was that she didn't have to drive all the time as she had done before returning to her hometown. She could get ready in the morning and, after a ten-minute walk, be entering the door of her classroom at Candle Beach Elementary.

Driving to Seattle by herself wouldn't be fun, but like she'd told Dahlia, a bright spot was that she'd have plenty of time to listen to audiobooks without a passenger critiquing her choice of reading material. With that in mind, she turned on the audiobook that she'd purchased from To Be Read and tried to relax as she pulled out of the driveway of the small house she'd been renting for the last few years.

The distraction worked, and she soon found herself nearing Seattle. She turned off the book, so she could focus on her phone's GPS as it read her directions to the university. Although she'd attended classes there for the last two years, she still had trouble locating the building on campus where the class would be held. Soon though, she was parking in front of a three-story stone building with a massive black iron door.

Inside, two women sat behind a long table, checking people in. A few people that she didn't recognize stood nearby, reviewing their paperwork.

"Sarah Rigg," Sarah said to the women as she approached the table.

The woman in front of her consulted her list, then placed a check mark on it with a green highlighter. "Great. I've got you all checked in." She motioned to the other woman at the table. "Susan will give you your lodging information and class schedule."

"Thank you." Sarah turned to the other woman, who handed her a sheet of paper.

"Here's the address for the dormitory, and you'll have classes in this building, of course. The schedule is on the back." She flipped through a small file box with dividers until she reached the "R" section and plucked out a plastic key card. "Here you go. This is what you'll use for your room and it will get you into the meal hall as well."

Sarah took it, examining the card. She ran her fingers along the smooth edge of the smart card with an embedded chip. Things had come a long way from the metal room keys she remembered from college.

The woman pointed to the side where a man was fiddling with a camera and lighting. "Joseph will help you with your temporary ID. Once you get that, you'll be all set."

"Thank you." Sarah walked over to the photographer and gave him her information. After being blinded by the flash, she received a rather unattractive photo of herself printed on another hard-plastic card. Good thing it was only a temporary ID card. She wasn't normally that concerned about her appearance, but the photographer had caught her blinking and she looked like an escapee from the state mental hospital.

"Sarah," someone called out. She whipped around to see who it was. Patrick. He grinned at her, displaying dimples in both of his cheeks. His dark hair flopped over his forehead, giving him a boyish look that seemed appropriate for the campus setting. He'd probably have half the female students who remained there for the summer falling all over him, but they'd be sorely disappointed to find out he had a fiancee.

She flushed. She shouldn't be thinking about Patrick in those terms either. *Keep it together, Sarah. Remember, he's engaged.*

She smiled at him. "Hey, how's it going?"

"Going great," he said with an easy grin. "I hope the instructor this year is as good as last year."

"Me too." She grimaced. "I took a class one time where the teacher spoke in a monotone voice and almost killed us with PowerPoint presentations. There wasn't much class participation. Even with guzzling cups of coffee and downing sugar during breaks, I found myself nodding off at times."

He laughed, a pleasant sound that made her want to laugh along with him. "Well, I hope that doesn't happen in this one." He nodded to the plastic badge clutched in her right hand. "Are you all set to head off to the dorms?"

"I am. My stuff is in the car though." She wanted to kick herself. Of course her things were in the car if she hadn't gone to the dorms yet.

"How about we drop off our luggage in our dorm rooms and head on down to the cafeteria?" He winked at her. "We can pretend we're carefree college students again."

That sounded pretty good to her. It seemed like ages ago that she'd allowed herself a moment away from her meticulous plans. Most of her time was dedicated to working, her family, and her classroom. Had she ever been a carefree college student?

She regarded him. He may not be her Mr. Right, but he might be a good friend. They'd hung out together the year before in a larger group setting, but she hadn't spent much time alone with him. "Sure. I'd like that."

They walked out to the parking lot together, chatting about their drives into the city.

He stopped in front of a vehicle a few cars down from hers and gestured to her Civic. "I thought that might be your car."

"How'd you know?" She scanned her car. Nothing on it screamed Candle Beach.

He pointed at the College of the Pacific bumper sticker on her back window. "I remembered you'd gone to college there. You don't see it mentioned much up here in Washington and you said you'd be here again this year."

"Ah." She hadn't even remembered telling him about where she'd attended college. He must have a good memory. "Yeah, I really don't meet many other alumni around here. Where did you go to college?"

"University of Puget Sound," he said, naming a college in Tacoma, a town south of Seattle.

She nodded. "I had a few friends that went there. Since we both went to smaller schools, this campus probably seems huge to you too." She spread her arms wide in two directions. As far as she could see, there were buildings associated with the University of Washington.

"No kidding. The grounds are massive." He opened his car door. "I'll meet you in the dorm lobby in thirty minutes for lunch, okay? We can get lost on campus together, just like we were freshmen again."

She got into her car, thinking about how fun it was to hang out with Patrick again. He was just so easy to be around and talk to, probably because he was attached to someone else and she didn't need to worry about there being any chance of a romantic relationship in their future. He was a good person to have as a friend. But if she was going to choose the perfect match for herself, he'd be a lot like Patrick – sweet, funny, handsome and witty. If only he had a twin brother.

They arrived at the dormitory at the same time.

"We meet again," he quipped as they entered the building together, dragging their wheeled suitcases behind them. The wheels slid smoothly on the vinyl faux hardwood flooring.

"Which floor are you on?" Sarah consulted the sheet of paper the woman had given her at registration. "I'm on fifth."

"Uh," he said, running his index finger over the lines on the paper. "Looks like I'm on floor six." He punched the up button on the wall to call the elevator to the first floor and they waited patiently as one came down from the twentieth floor.

"Even the dorms are huge here," Sarah whispered. "The whole student population from my college could have fit into one of these dorms."

The elevator pinged, and they rolled their suitcases in.

She leaned against the wall of the elevator as they watched the floor numbers go up.

"Floor five," he announced like an elevator operator. "Enjoy your stay, miss." He tipped a fake hat at her and she giggled like a little girl before covering her mouth.

"I will, thank you so much, kind sir." She moved out of the elevator and broke character. "I'll see you downstairs after I get settled."

He barely had time to nod before the elevator doors closed, cutting her off from him and leaving her alone. After their friendly banter, the hallway was eerily quiet. She quickly found her room and tapped the plastic key card against the rectangular black reader affixed to the wall. The indicator turned green and she turned the door handle.

Whereas last year they'd been housed in an older dorm with individual rooms and bathrooms down the hall, this year she'd been assigned a room in a pod-style dorm apartment, with four single bedrooms off of a small kitchen and living room. Between the two bedrooms on each side was a full bathroom with a shower and tub combo. If she had roommates for the next few days, none of them had arrived yet. She set her luggage in one of the rooms and walked over to the living room window.

From the fifth floor, she had a bird's-eye view of much of the campus. She could only imagine what it would look like from the twentieth floor. From there, she could probably see halfway to Candle Beach, or to Canada. At the thought of Candle Beach, she felt instantly homesick, which was ridiculous considering she'd only been away from home for a few hours. She'd tried life away from the beach for a few years, but the only thing that felt right to her was to move back to her hometown. She'd never regretted that decision, although it definitely hadn't done anything good for her love life.

Sarah glanced at her watch. She'd been checking out the view for so long that she was due to meet Patrick in the lobby in five minutes. After fixing her travel-mussed hair in the bathroom mirror, she hurried downstairs, but he wasn't there yet.

Patrick came up behind her while she was reading some of the posters on a bulletin board and tapped her on the shoulder.

She whirled around. "Hey," she said, then realized he wasn't alone. A tall man with thinning hair smiled down at her.

"This is my roomie, Andrew," Patrick said. "Andrew, this is my friend, Sarah."

Andrew nodded, and she smiled back at him, but Patrick's introduction of her as his friend stabbed into her. Not that she was anything but a friend to him, but it was becoming clearer every day that she was tired of always being the friend. Her college friends were all married already, and some were having kids. She was still stuck in a rental house in her hometown, alone.

At least she'd made friends in the last few months. She'd accepted the job at To Be Read because she wanted to earn more money to pad her nest egg, but it had given her so much more. Now, she considered Dahlia, the bookstore owner, and Charlotte, who lived in the apartment above the store, to be two of her closest friends. But even they were both in serious relationships.

"Hey, are you there?" Patrick waved his hand in front of her face.

She focused her attention on him, heat rising up her neck from being caught daydreaming. "Yeah, sorry."

"I told Andrew we were going to grab a bite to eat in the cafeteria and he asked to join us."

"Sure, that's great. The more the merrier." She cast a glance at Andrew's hand but didn't see a wedding band. Was he single? As soon as the thought crossed her mind, she felt as though she were in someone else's body. She'd never gone through life worrying about finding a boyfriend. She'd always had too much to do and goals to accomplish.

But this was what happened to a person when almost everyone they knew was happily coupled up. Or maybe, as she entered her early thirties, her biological clock was ticking. "Do you remember where it's at?"

Patrick nodded. "It's a few blocks away. I hope they're serving something good today because I'm starving."

As they walked, she asked Andrew, "So where are you from?"

"Dunley Hills. It's a small town outside of Portland. And you?"

"I'm from Candle Beach on the Washington Coast."

Not surprisingly, he gave her a quizzical look.

"It's about half an hour north of Haven Shores," she explained.

Recognition dawned on his face. "Ah. I've never been to that part of the coast, but I hear it's beautiful."

A warmth flooded over her. "It is." She smiled at him. "What grade do you teach?"

"Fourth," he said. "It's a fun age. They're not so little anymore, but they don't think they know everything yet like middle schoolers."

She laughed. "I teach fourth too and I know what you mean."

Beside her, Patrick was rather quiet. He'd been so talkative earlier, but she couldn't tell if something was wrong now.

"Here we are," he said. "The union building."

The cafeteria offered a buffet-style serving during the summer, so they swiped their meal cards and went through the lines in search of edible food.

When the three of them sat down at a long rectangular table together, Sarah burst out laughing.

"What?" Patrick asked.

"This is so much like when I was back in college." She pointed at their trays, which were full of cookies and grilled cheese sandwiches. "No wonder I gained the famous freshman fifteen."

Andrew chuckled. "I see what you mean." He gave them a sheepish grin. "When I'm at home, my wife always makes me eat healthy, so when I'm away, I indulge a little."

Sarah's gut twisted. Of course he was married. The good ones always were.

"I usually eat fairly healthy too, but when you're on vacation..." She smiled and took a bite of creamy macaroni and cheese.

The three of them spent the next twenty minutes talking about their classrooms and their plans for the upcoming school year. Patrick's demeanor had brightened, and he was acting much more interested in the conversation. They were in the midst of a lively discussion about the funniest things kids had ever done in their classes when Andrew's phone rang.

He glanced at it. With a guilty look, he said, "It's my wife. I completely forgot that I was supposed to call her when I got here." He stood from the table. "It was nice meeting you both. I'll see you tomorrow in class, Sarah." He turned to Patrick. "And I'll see you back in the apartment."

"See you later," Patrick said.

"Nice meeting you too." Sarah smiled at him. Andrew left, talking on his phone as he walked.

"I hope he's not in too much trouble with his wife." Patrick took a bite of the last chocolate chip cookie on his plate, then set it down and wiped his mouth with a paper napkin.

"I'm sure he's fine." Sarah pushed her plate away before she was tempted to eat more macaroni and cheese than her stomach could handle. "That is, as long as we don't tell her about the junk food."

He laughed. "So, what's going on with you?" He picked up the cookie again and finished it in a few bites. "You're still teaching in Candle Beach, right?"

She nodded. "Yeah, still teaching at the same school, in the same classroom." Her life sounded even more boring when she uttered it out loud than it did when she thought about it. "I'm thinking about buying a house there though."

His eyebrows lifted. "That's great. Doesn't most of your family live there?"

He really had remembered a lot about her from last summer.

"Yes, my older brother Adam, and my older sister Jenny and her family, as well as my parents, all live in Candle Beach. We Riggs don't stray far from the beach."

"It must be nice to have so much family around. Mine is all in the Midwest."

"Really? How did you end up in the Northwest?" With a start, she realized that although she'd known him for a year, she actually knew very little about him – much less than he knew about her.

He laughed. "Well, after I graduated from college there weren't a lot of teaching jobs around, so I applied for every position I could find on the West Coast. Haven Shores was the first one on the list that called me back and offered me a job." His eyes took on a far-off look. "It's funny though, I've really come to love the place. I think small-town life suits me."

"Oh yeah, weren't you remodeling a house in Haven Shores?" The idea of taking an old house and making it beautiful again appealed to her, but she didn't have the technical skills to pull it off.

"I am still in the process of renovations." His eyes twinkled. "But I'm on my third house in Haven Shores since I moved there. I think I'd just bought this one last year when I met you."

Her eyes stretched wide. "Oh, so you're flipping houses."

"Well, I wouldn't say that I'm flipping them." He laughed self-consciously. "The concept of flipping a house always has such negative connotations. I'm not purely in it for the money, although that's a nice side benefit. I've found that renovating houses is something I'm good at and that I enjoy immensely. Seeing a house go from run-down to beautifully restored and knowing that I'm the one that made it happen is a wonderful feeling."

"I can see how that would be nice." She fiddled with her napkin. It was too bad that the house he was remodeling was in Haven Shores. She'd love to have a newly remodeled vintage home. Then again, the price point would probably be much higher than anything she could ever hope to afford.

As if he'd read her mind, he asked, "Hey, are you interested in buying a house in Haven Shores? I might know someone who'll have a house on the market in a few months." He winked at her.

She laughed. "No, I'd like to stay up in Candle Beach. I

really dislike driving, so I like living close to work." She stared off at a distant point in the cafeteria. "Anyway, I'm not even sure that I'm going to buy a house anytime soon."

"Why not?" He stared at her as though she were crazy.

She sighed. "Well, it's just me. I don't have any plans of getting married anytime soon and the idea of taking on a large mortgage on a teacher's salary is a little intimidating."

"I understand what you mean about taking on the mortgage, but I'm sure it will work out for you." He sipped from his glass of water, then set it down on the table.

"Do you really think so?" She'd run the numbers over and over again and even with a second job at the bookstore, it would be tight. She didn't want to get in over her head like some people had when the housing market crashed.

"I do." He stood from the table and picked up his tray. "I mean, look at me. I'm on a teacher's salary as well and I'm on my third house."

"I guess." His house renovating business wasn't exactly the same thing because she wasn't able to do the work herself if something went wrong with a house.

"Besides, I doubt you'll stay single for very long." He added quickly, "Not that you have to be in a relationship to buy a house."

She looked up and laughed harshly. "The suitors aren't exactly banging down my door. I'm a teacher in a small town and most everyone I know is already married, or well on their way to a wedding. I never meet anyone that I'm interested in. Maybe I'm too picky." She slumped a little, then forced herself to stand up, picking up her tray in the process. "Sorry. I shouldn't be telling you all this. It makes me sound really pathetic."

Patrick appeared to be thinking about what she said. "You know, I have a friend in Haven Shores that might be perfect for you." He searched her face. "Do you mind if I give him your phone number?"

Did she mind? She stared at Patrick. If his friend was anything like him, she was sure they would make a good match. The last time someone had tried to set her up, it had fallen through before she even met the man. This arrangement had to be better than that.

"Um. I guess that would be okay."

They walked over to the tray return area and left the cafeteria.

"Are you really okay with me giving my friend your contact info?"

Was she? She peeked at him in her peripheral vision as they walked. Why couldn't Patrick himself be available? His fiancée was a lucky woman.

"Yes. That's fine." She forced a smile. "I'd love to meet him."

"Great." He went quiet again, barely speaking to her until they'd entered the dorm lobby. "Well, I'll see you later. Give me a call if you want to have dinner together later."

"I'll do that." She scrutinized his face. Why was he acting so distant?

They rode up together in the elevator and he said goodbye when they reached her floor, but his demeanor was flat. Had she done something wrong? She shook her head. She hoped she hadn't offended him somehow because she didn't have many male friends and Patrick seemed like he'd make a good friend.

a week after the course ended, Sarah stood in the back of her classroom admiring the décor. She'd been working hard all week in between shifts at the bookstore to make her room a welcoming place for the incoming fourth graders.

"I like it," her friend Maura said from the doorway. Maura's dark brown hair swished around her shoulders as she turned her head to view the whole room. "You added a rug to the reading nook, and new pillows."

"I saw the rug at a department store in Haven Shores for half off and couldn't resist." Sarah walked over to the green rug with a border of purple flowers. "It looked like something out of The Secret Garden."

A book had fallen off the bookshelf, so she knelt down on the rug, her knees sinking into the plush fibers. She carefully reshelved the book and stood, eying the rest of the room for anything out of place. The school didn't give the teachers much money for decorating their classroom, so she usually ended up spending some of her own funds, but it was worth it. The kids were going to love it.

"How's your office?" Sarah asked.

"Not much has changed since last year." Maura laughed. "I did get a new "hang in there" poster for the wall."

Maura had been a guidance counselor at Bluebonnet Middle School next door for the whole time Sarah had been teaching in Candle Beach. Sarah had seen Maura crocheting in the shared middle school/elementary school staff room and had asked her to teach her how to crochet a blanket for her then baby niece. They'd bonded over crochet patterns and had been good friends ever since.

"How was that class you took in Seattle? Did you enjoy it as much as last year?"

The first thing that came to mind when Sarah thought about her drama class was the way the skin around Patrick's eyes crinkled adorably while he was telling a joke. Her face flushed, thinking about how much she'd enjoyed spending time with him during the multi-day class. She tried to regain her composure, but Maura caught her reaction before she could do so.

Maura narrowed her eyes at Sarah. "Why are you blushing?"

"I'm not," Sarah said, willing her complexion to return to its normal color.

"You are." Maura leaned against the doorframe. "Did something happen at the class? Did you meet a nice guy there?"

"Well, no. I mean, yes, I did hang out with a male friend I made last year and his roommate while I was there, but neither of them are single." She had gone to dinner with Andrew and Patrick all three nights of their stay and she'd had a wonderful time with them. She'd almost forgotten what male companionship was like, even if it was completely platonic. But it had been completely platonic, so why was she acting like it wasn't?

Heat crept up her neck again and she fanned herself. "It's hot in here. I wish they'd turn the air-conditioning on if they expect us to be here the week before school starts."

Maura looked at her dubiously. "I think the thermostat outside my room said it was seventy-one degrees. Maybe you're having a hot flash."

"It's not a hot flash! I'm barely thirty. Maybe it's hotter on this side of the building than it is on yours." Sarah walked over to her desk and took a long drink from her reusable water bottle. The ice cubes she'd stuck in there earlier had done their job and the chilled water slid down her throat, cooling her immensely.

"Probably." Maura eyed her again. "So, did you have a good time in Seattle?"

"I did." Sarah smiled. "The class was interesting. I was afraid it might be a repeat of what we learned last year, but this one was more advanced, and I learned some new techniques. I'm looking forward to sharing them with my class and maybe putting on a short play in the spring."

"Sounds fun. Anything else new with you?"

"Um." Sarah thought for a moment. "I'm thinking about buying a house in Candle Beach."

"You are?" Maura squealed. "That's so awesome. You'll love it and you will finally have room for your yarn collection."

Sarah laughed. "I'll need a second bedroom just for yarn at the rate we've been going." She and Maura had gone on a yarn crawl a few weeks ago and visited several fiber shops along the coast. The result had been way more skeins of yarn than she could possibly use in the next few years. They were currently stuffed into the top shelf of her bedroom closet, but her collection kept spilling over and hitting her on the head every time she opened the closet door.

It would be nice to have more space. Her one-bedroom house was nice enough, but no one could call it spacious. In fact, her brother Adam had once called it her hobbit hole because of the arched back door and small interior square footage.

"I don't know though." She moved some books around on her desk. "Buying a house is a big deal."

"Yeah, but this is where you want to settle, right?"

"Yes, but I never thought I'd be buying a house on my own."

Maura waved her hand in the air. "You'll be fine."

"That's what Patrick said." Sarah quickly shut her mouth, realizing her friend would pounce on his name.

She didn't disappoint. "Who's Patrick?"

"My friend from the class – the attached one," Sarah said pointedly.

Maura nodded, surprising her by letting the mention of Patrick pass. Evidently the prospect of her buying a home was even more important than the possibility of a new man in Sarah's life. "Okay, so what did he say?"

Sarah sighed. "He said I should go for it. He buys houses all the time and remodels them for fun though. I don't know how to do any of that."

Maura shrugged. "So? You'll learn, and you'll buy a house that isn't a fixer-upper. Problem solved."

"What about if the district has to downsize teachers? If my contract isn't renewed next year I won't be able to make my mortgage payments." Lawnmower engines roared outside, and the sweet smell of freshly mowed grass filtered in through the open window as the maintenance staff prepared the grounds for school starting next week. Her brain whirred so quickly that her thoughts threatened to drown out all sounds from outside. There were so many things that could go wrong.

"You can't think about everything that could go wrong," Maura said, echoing her thoughts. "You'll go crazy if you do."

"But that doesn't mean they won't happen," she said stubbornly.

"And it doesn't mean they will." Maura sighed. "With the best things that can happen in your life, sometimes you just have to leap."

"I guess." The idea of buying a house was really starting to gel in her brain but it was such a big undertaking. Her friends were all telling her to go for it, so why was she so nervous? Sometimes she wished she could jump into things without thinking them through completely, but that had never been her style. Even as a kid, she'd watch the other children playing a new game on the playground and wouldn't join in until she'd first figured out all the rules.

"Anything new with you?" she asked Maura.

"Nope," Maura said. "My summer was pretty boring. I went to California for a week to visit my parents, but other than that, I stayed home and puttered around the house."

"And I thought I was boring," Sarah said in a teasing voice.

"Hey!" Maura exclaimed. "Hold your punches." She sobered. "But seriously, I'm starting to think I need to sign up for one of those dating apps. That's the only way I'm going to meet someone around here."

"Well, don't take the last available man," Sarah said. Secretly though, she was a little happy that she wasn't the only one who wasn't in a relationship. And if Maura, with her long dark hair and classic good looks, wasn't dating anyone there must be pretty slim pickings in the area.

"Don't worry, I won't. And if I do meet someone, I'll make sure he has a brother for you, deal?"

"Deal." Sarah grabbed her purse and keys off the desk and walked toward the door. "I'd better get going. I have a shift this afternoon at To Be Read."

"Me too. I've got a hot date with a baby blanket for my nephew." Maura exited the room first and Sarah locked the door behind them.

5

*P*atrick leaned back in his chair and kicked his feet up on the footrest in front of him, gazing out at puffy clouds floating high over the ocean. He sighed and took a swig from the bottle of beer he'd set on the glass outdoor end table. A hummingbird hovered over a flowering bush next to the deck, its wings moving in a mesmerizing pattern. He felt the stress melt out of his body. This was the life.

"Comfortable?" Parker asked as he walked out onto the deck with a bowl of chips. "You look like you're about to move in."

Patrick laughed. "Sorry. I'm a little sore from crawling around on the floor in my house, working on the baseboards. It feels good to sit out here in the sun and relax a little. And you can't beat this view." The afternoon sun felt wonderful as it soaked through the fabric of his jeans and warmed his aching muscles. "Thanks for inviting me over."

"Yeah, no problem. Gretchen went out of town for a friend's baby shower and I'm all by myself for a few days."

"So you're saying I'm second best," Patrick said in a deadpan voice.

Parker stared at him, his hand holding his beer bottle frozen in mid-air.

"I'm joking." Patrick laughed at his friend's expression. "I really appreciate this. School starts soon and then my days will be full. It's nice to spend time hanging out with a friend before my life returns to the chaos that is the school year." He dipped a chip in the bowl of salsa Parker had set on the glass patio table in front of them.

"Have you given any more thought to selling your house?" Parker asked.

Patrick chewed slowly, giving himself more time to think. "I don't know. I want to say yes, but I don't want to be hurried either and I'm not sure how much time I'll be able to devote to finishing the house once school starts." It was a big decision and he still wasn't entirely certain that he wanted to move on from his dream house quite yet.

Parker nodded. "My client is still interested. I'll let them know about your reservations and see what they want to do."

"How is business going?" Patrick asked.

"Good." Parker beamed. "Gretchen and I are making a name for ourselves in the area and we've got new clients signing on every day. What about you? Are you looking forward to school starting?"

Patrick shrugged. "I like meeting the new kids in my class and watching them learn throughout the year, but sometimes it's not that exciting. I've been teaching fifth grade for close to ten years now and I pretty much have my lesson plan down pat. Although, I took a class recently about introducing dramatic arts and I think I'll try some of the techniques out this year. Maybe that will liven things up." He swiveled around to look toward the side yard leading to the street in front of Parker's house. "One of my classmates was from Candle Beach actually."

"Oh, really?" Parker asked. "Who? It's a small town, I probably know them."

"Sarah Rigg. She's a teacher at the elementary school."

Parker smiled. "I do know Sarah. She's friends with Gretchen's group of friends. I think they're going to need to start calling themselves the Candle Beach Women's Club because they're always meeting up at the local wine bar and hanging out together, just like the older women in town who call themselves the Ladies of Candle Beach."

"She's nice," Patrick said carefully, his heart quickening at the thought of Sarah. Her warm brunette hair and engaging smile made his throat catch every time he saw her. Unfortunately, she only saw him as a friend.

"She is." Parker looked at him. "Are you interested in her?"

He shook his head. "No, no. We're just friends." He remembered his promise to her to give his friend her phone number. "In fact, I was thinking about fixing her up with a friend of mine."

Parker laughed. "I hope her luck with a blind date this time is better than what happened to her last time."

"What's that?" When he'd spoken with her about his friend, Sarah hadn't mentioned being set up before.

"My sister, Charlotte, was supposed to set Sarah up with someone – my childhood best friend, actually – and she accidentally fell in love with him herself. Sarah still teases her about it."

"Wow, that's rough." He was quiet for a moment. "No, my friend is a nice guy. I think they'll hit it off."

"Good," Parker said. "Sarah deserves to be happy."

"Uh-huh." Patrick looked up at the sky. For some reason, the idea of Sarah being happy with another guy was really eating at him. She'd made it clear she had no interest in him, so he needed to get over any feelings he had for her ASAP. "Have you set a wedding date yet?"

"Yes, we're planning on getting married in December. You should get a wedding invitation soon. Gretchen's handling all of that."

"Great. I'm happy for you, man. She sounds like a great girl."

"She is." Parker grinned. "Now we just need to find someone for you."

Patrick held his hand up. "Wait just a minute here. Just because you found the perfect girl doesn't mean there's one waiting for me somewhere." He shook his head. "I've been down that road before. At this point, I'm probably better off staying single."

Parker eyed him. "Don't let your experience with Nina color your entire future. Not all women are like that."

He sighed. "I know. For now though, I think I'm going to focus on remodeling the house and teaching my fifth grade class this year. Those should keep me busy enough."

"Sounds pretty boring."

Patrick shot him a mock glare. It may be boring, but it decreased his chance of being hurt again.

"Say, I've been thinking," Parker said. "Would you be interested in taking on a partner in your renovation business?"

He looked at Parker. He'd never really thought of it as a business, more like a hobby where he made some extra cash once in a while. "Why, are you interested?"

Parker nodded. "I've been thinking about branching out into investing in real estate myself – not just selling it."

"Really." He was silent for a minute, thinking about Parker's offer. "So how would it work?"

"I was thinking that we could go in on the properties together and you'd be in charge of the renovation with limited input from me. We could figure out an equitable way to split the profits since you'd be putting in more of the day-to-day work on the houses."

"That could work," Patrick said slowly. "But I'm not the type of person that can just slap some paint on a house and call it good. When I choose a house to work on, I want to be able to bring it back to its original glory. No cutting corners."

Parker nodded vigorously. "I completely agree. There are plenty of clients out there who want completely renovated houses from the early 1900s and they're willing to pay for it. You wouldn't need to cut corners in quality."

A wide smile stretched across Patrick's face. This project with Parker might be just what he needed to get out of the funk he'd been in since Nina left.

He held out his hand. "Let's make this work, partner."

Parker grasped his hand and shook it. "Okay, partner."

They stood there for a moment, grinning like fools.

Parker cleared his throat. "Hey, it's getting late. Do you want to walk over to the pub and grab some hot wings? I think there's a game on tonight too."

"Sure, I'd like that." They brought their snacks and empty bottles into the kitchen, then set out for the pub on Main Street. The sidewalks were full of tourists ambling slowly down the concrete, chattering away while enjoying pre-dinner ice cream cones. Luckily, the pub wasn't too busy yet. He'd never spent too much time up in Candle Beach, but it was a cute town and he was interested in seeing more of it.

Receiving an invitation to become business partners

hadn't been what Patrick had expected when Parker invited him over for beers, but he couldn't have been more pleased. With his friend's investment, he'd be able to take on more projects than he could before and not have to worry so much about any financial implications. It would be a winning situation for both of them.

A week after school started, Sarah's cell phone rang while she was making dinner, cutting off the nineties easy listening station she'd been listening to via her phone.

"Hello?" she asked, the phone pressed tight against her ear as she continued to chop onions for French onion soup. A tidy pile of sliced onions sat in a navy-blue glass bowl off to the side. Only three more to go.

"Hi Sarah, it's Patrick."

Her heart raced at the sound of his voice and she forced herself to calm down. "Oh, hi." An onion-induced tear escaped her eye and she set the knife down to brush it away.

"I was calling because I gave my friend Derek your phone number and he said he'd be calling you. I wanted to give you a heads-up about it first."

He still wanted to set her up with his friend? She hesitated, then said, "Thanks for letting me know."

"He's a great guy," Patrick reassured her.

"I'm looking forward to meeting him." More tears sprang from her eyes and she sniffled to keep her nose from running. She loved to cook, but onions made her cry every time she used them. Her last apartment's kitchen had a fan over the prep area, which had helped, but her rental house's tiny kitchen had cupboards above all of the counter space.

"Are you okay?" His voice was full of alarm. "You sound like you're crying."

"Uh-huh. I'm chopping onions for dinner. I love French onion soup, but preparing it always makes me cry." She held the phone away from her face while she swiped at her eyes and nose with a Kleenex.

He laughed, and she could picture his dimpled smile through the phone line. "Okay, I won't keep you any longer. I wanted to ask you though – do you want to grab a coffee sometime and compare notes on how we're using drama in the classroom? I'd love another local teacher's input on the program I have planned for my students."

"Sure, that would be great."

"You sound busy right now, so I'll give you a call later to set something up. I hope your soup turns out delicious. I'll talk to you later."

"Bye." She hung up the phone and set it down on the counter in front of her, her stomach churning with a mixture of excitement and nausea. The music station turned back on now that the call was over and Savage Garden came on singing about being truly, madly, deeply in love.

She wanted to find love like that, but did she really want to be set up on a blind date? It was a little late to back out though, if Patrick's friend was already planning to call. And maybe he'd be just as great as Patrick. Wasn't that what she was hoping for? Her stomach flip-flopped again, but whether it was from nerves, or the pervasive onion odor in her kitchen, she didn't know.

6

---

*P*atrick's friend Derek had called her to set up a date and they'd settled on a movie at the theater in Haven Shores followed by dinner. Since he lived in Haven Shores, she'd told him that she'd meet him at the movie theater.

When she arrived, she scanned the parking lot, looking for a man of medium height with sandy-blond hair. She saw a possible candidate walking along the sidewalk, searching for someone. She hurried over to him.

"Are you Derek?" she asked.

His eyes lit up, as though he liked what he saw. "Yes. Sarah?"

She nodded. "I was worried I wouldn't be able to find you. I didn't realize it was opening night for the latest super-hero movie."

"Me neither." He flashed her a grin full of pearly-white teeth. "Do you want to do something else?"

"No, this is fine." She pushed her way through the crowd until she was close enough to read the names of the movies that were playing. "What do you think about the romantic comedy?" She pointed at the sign. "It's playing at six o'clock."

A look of pain shot across his face, but he smiled. "The romantic comedy it is."

It obviously wasn't his first choice and she didn't want him to hate the movie.

"Are you sure?"

"Of course. If that's what you want to see, it's fine with me."

"Okay." She shot him a dubious look, but he went to the counter and came back with tickets for the next show. They walked inside, and Sarah glanced at the concession stand. To her, the movie theater popcorn was always the best thing about attending a movie in a theater.

"Did you want to get something?" he asked. "I thought we might skip it since we're going to eat dinner afterward."

He had a point, but the aroma of butter and freshly popped corn was too enticing.

"Maybe just a small container of popcorn?" She smiled. "I love it."

"A small container it is." They stood in line and he paid for a small popcorn and a soda for her and a bottle of water for himself. She offered to pay, but he refused her money.

When they were seated she offered him some popcorn.

"No thanks, I try not to put anything like that in my body. I'm in training for a marathon."

She noticed for the first time that there wasn't an ounce of fat on his body.

"A marathon? That's great."

The previews started, and the crowd hushed.

"You'll have to tell me about the marathon at dinner," she whispered to him.

He nodded, then turned his attention to the screen.

He seemed standoffish, but she assumed it was because they'd just met. Although he was good-looking, she didn't feel an instant attraction to him or a sense of ease when she was with him. Hopefully that would get better at dinner, because she really wanted the date to go well. She was tired of being one of the only single people in her group of friends.

When the movie ended, she stood, but he motioned for her to sit back down.

"The credits are still rolling," he whispered.

He didn't see her raise her eyebrows because his attention was fixed on the movie screen. Finally, the screen went dark. She glanced at him to see if he was ready to go.

He rose quickly then strode to the back of the theater, as if expecting her to follow. When they were outside the theater, he stopped near a tree.

"What did you have in mind for dinner?" she asked, almost afraid to find out.

"I was thinking the vegetarian buffet on Eighth Street."

Her stomach rumbled. She'd been leaning toward a steak or something. She hadn't had time for lunch and the popcorn had only served to whet her appetite.

"Uh, maybe we could get something heartier?"

He sighed. "Everyone always has so many misconceptions about vegetarian food. It's very filling."

That may be true, but it wasn't a steak. "How about we go to the Thai restaurant down the street? I saw it on the way in. They'll probably have tofu or other vegetarian dishes you could eat." She could almost taste the beef pad khee mao noodles and tom kha coconut milk soup.

He stared up at the sky and then back down to her. "Fine. We can do that."

"Do you want to walk? It's a beautiful night." The street-lights were on and the air was fresh and crisp.

"Sure. Always good to get more exercise."

She breathed a sigh of relief. Finally, she'd come up with an idea that he didn't hate. This wasn't the worse date she'd ever been on, but it certainly wasn't the best. How had she ever thought that he might have been just like Patrick?

They walked down the street toward the Thai restaurant together, but she fought for something to say to him.

"The leaves are gorgeous, aren't they?" She waved her hand at the orange, red and yellow leaves that were scattered on the sidewalk and street. "This is one of my favorite times of year."

He nodded. "I prefer spring though. I'm not a fan of fall because of all of the holiday nonsense. I mean seriously, I can't even go into a store without Halloween, Thanksgiving, and Christmas being shoved at me from all directions."

Her eyes widened. What kind of person didn't like Christmas? She'd better not tell him about the four boxes of Christmas decorations she had packed away in a storage room in the basement – or that she planned on putting them up soon.

They arrived at the Thai restaurant and he opened the door for her.

"Table for two?" the hostess asked, menus in hand.

Derek nodded curtly. The hostess seated them near the kitchen.

"Can we move to a different table? I really don't like being near all that noise," he said.

"Of course, sir." She led them over to a different table, in the opposite corner of the restaurant.

Sarah couldn't help but wonder if they'd make it out of the restaurant without one of the chefs or waitstaff spitting in their food. Maybe they would have been better off with the vegetarian place.

When they were seated and had ordered, the silence between them was deafening.

"So, what did you think of the movie?" Sarah sipped from the Thai iced coffee the waitress had brought her.

"Eh," he said. "It was rather formulaic."

She stared at him. "It's a romantic comedy. They're supposed to be formulaic. It's all about the relationships between the main characters."

"I suppose, but I think a different movie would have been better." He leaned forward to drain half of his glass of water with his straw.

She didn't know what to say. He'd agreed to the movie and he hadn't wanted to leave until the credits were over with. Now he was saying it was awful? She felt nauseous. This guy definitely wasn't like Patrick.

"So, what do you do for work?" she asked politely, wishing that the kitchen staff could prepare their food more quickly.

He puffed up. "I'm a banker with First Shores bank."

"Oh. That must be, um...interesting. Do you get much contact with clients?"

"I do." He smiled. "I help them with loans and investing for the future."

He seemed to actually enjoy his job and she warmed a little to him as he told her more about his position at the bank. Soon, the waitress brought their food.

She dug into her five-star spicy pad khee mao and swooned. "This is delicious."

He looked at her food and grimaced. "I don't know how you can eat such spicy food. It's not good for your digestion."

Her fork stopped midway to her mouth. Why did he

insist on being so negative? She shrugged. "I happen to like it this way and I've never encountered any stomach issues from spicy foods." To prove her point, she shoveled the food into her mouth and made a show of how good it tasted.

He just shook his head and put a bite of brown rice and tofu into his mouth. Her brother Adam always teased her about having a cast-iron stomach but, for some reason, Derek's words didn't seem like teasing in good fun like Adam's.

"Patrick tells me you're a teacher."

She set down her fork and felt enthusiastic for the first time that evening. "Yes. I've been teaching since I graduated from college almost ten years ago. I started out in first grade, but I've moved up to fourth grade now, which I love."

"Doesn't it get boring being around little kids all day?"

Boring? Did he hate kids too in addition to all of his other bad qualities? This was quickly sinking into worst-date-ever territory.

She flashed him a grin. "Nope. I love teaching. Their minds are like sponges, soaking up everything I can offer them. There's something special about that."

"Hmm. I couldn't handle being a teacher. My own nieces and nephews are stressful enough to be around."

"Oh." She looked down at her food and picked out the last piece of chicken in her soup. She chewed it slowly to give her time away from talking to him, enjoying the creaminess of the coconut milk, the tang of lime and lemongrass and the savoriness from a generous dose of fish sauce. So far, discovering this restaurant had been the only good thing about this date.

"How is everything going?" their waitress asked as she stood in front of their table. "Does everything taste okay?"

She looked pointedly at Derek, who'd barely touched his food.

"It's delicious," Sarah said before he could say anything.

The waitress smiled at her, glanced at Derek, and rushed off before he could reply as well.

He frowned at Sarah. "I was going to tell her the rice was undercooked."

She sighed and surreptitiously pulled her cell phone out of her purse, glancing at it from under the table.

She tapped out a text to Maura. *SOS.* If she didn't get out of there soon, she was going to scream.

A minute later, Maura called.

"Oh, I'm so sorry to hear you're not feeling well. I'll be right there." Sarah hung up her phone, grabbed her purse, and stood from the table. "My friend isn't feeling well, and I need to go take care of her."

He looked up at her in surprise, as if he'd thought the date was going well. "Do you have to go so soon?"

She forced an expression of regret. "Yeah, sorry about that. She's really sick and she doesn't have anyone else to help take care of her."

He pushed the food aside and called the waitress over to get the bill. She hurried back with it and set it in the middle of the table. Sarah reached for it and handed the waitress her credit card.

"I'll take care of it. You got my food at the theater and you didn't seem to like this much."

He opened his mouth, as if to disagree, but then shrugged. "I'll buy you dinner next time."

Next time? Was he insane? There was definitely not going to be a next time, not even if he were the last man on earth. What had Patrick been thinking when he set her up with Derek? She'd thought she and Patrick had a good

45

connection, but maybe he didn't know her as well as she'd thought.

The waitress returned with the bill and credit card and Sarah signed for it, giving the waitress a nice tip for having to deal with Derek.

Sarah pressed her lips into a thin line and didn't address his remark about a second date. She could only hope he'd lose her phone number. "Well, thank you for a nice evening. Don't hurry out of here on my account." She scurried away as quickly as possible, almost sprinting to her car for fear that Derek would stop her.

She really did drive to Maura's house afterward but, of course, her friend wasn't sick.

"That bad?" Maura asked when she opened the door to Sarah.

Sarah nodded. "Yep. That bad."

Maura motioned for her to come in and offered her a glass of wine. As she handed the full glass to Sarah, she said, "Maybe the next time someone plays matchmaker, things will turn out better?"

"I'm never going out on another blind date." She sighed. "This was horrible. I seriously don't understand why Patrick would have set me up with him. We had nothing in common. I foolishly assumed that since they were friends, he might be like Patrick, but Patrick is so much friendlier, kinder and, above all, much more interesting."

Maura eyed her with a sly smile on her face. "Uh-huh. And of course, you have no interest in Patrick, right?"

"None. Besides, he's engaged." Sarah resolved that her assertion was true, or at least she'd do her best to make it true. There was no point obsessing over a happily-engaged man.

"Okay then." Maura changed the subject. "It's still fairly early. Do you want to grab dessert at the Bluebonnet Café?"

In her hurry to escape from Derek, Sarah hadn't finished her noodle dish at the Thai restaurant and she was still hungry. It had pained her to leave it on her plate and not get it to go, but any more time with Derek would have been too much.

"Dessert would be great. They'd better have something high calorie and chocolate though. I need that tonight."

Maura laughed. "Let's see if they have something that can drown out the memory of your bad date."

As she walked to the café with Maura, Sarah was suddenly grateful for the friends she'd made since returning to Candle Beach. She hoped to someday find her perfect match and build a family with him but, if she didn't, at least she had good friends.

7

A couple of weeks into the school year, Patrick called to invite her for coffee, to discuss how they were implementing what they'd learned about drama in their classrooms. Several of the kids in her class had a flair for the dramatic, so she had no doubt they'd love it if she came up with additional ideas to incorporate theater into their studies.

"Over here," he called out when Sarah arrived at the coffee shop in Haven Shores. He was sitting in a dark wooden chair at a table for two in the corner of the shop and she hadn't seen him at first. She waved to him and cut through the throngs of people, waiting to order, to get to where he was sitting.

"Hey," she said as she took off her coat. "I'm going to order a latte. Do you want anything?" She motioned to the crumb-filled paper napkin in front of him. He appeared to have been sitting there for quite some time already, although she was sure she wasn't late.

"No." He smiled that dimpled grin at her and her heart almost melted before she steeled herself against it. "I got here early and was working on some of my lesson plans, so I thought I'd grab a snack." He nodded behind her at the line. "You'd better get over there if you want to get your order sometime this year."

She groaned inwardly when she saw the line of people, which had doubled in the last few minutes and was now snaking across the coffee shop, almost to the door. She quickly took her place and, after taking a couple of minutes to decide what she wanted to order, she allowed her mind to wander.

Although her date with Derek had been a disaster, he'd called her afterward and invited her on a second date. She'd politely declined. What would Patrick think though? Would Derek have told him she'd turned down a second date? Patrick had seemed sincere in setting them up and she didn't want to hurt his feelings, so if Derek hadn't said anything to him, she wasn't going to either. Her vision drifted over to Patrick.

His head was bent over a notebook and she let her gaze linger on him. He scratched something on the paper with his ballpoint pen and absentmindedly took a sip out of his venti-sized coffee without looking up. Why was it that when she'd finally found a man that checked off all the boxes, he was engaged? What were the odds that she would find another kind man, who loved kids, made her laugh, and was easy to talk to? That was a tall order.

"Miss?" Someone broke into her reverie and she looked up to see the drawn face of an exhausted barista. He looked as though he needed a few shots of his own wares. Somehow she'd made it to the front of the line, mindlessly following the person in front of her without even noticing.

She shook her head. "Oh, sorry. I was lost in thought." She stared at the menu. All memories of what she'd planned to order had flown from her head when it filled with thoughts of the perfect man.

"What would you like?" the man asked, impatience seeping through every word. Someone behind her bumped her and she had to lean against the counter to catch her balance. The movement jolted her enough to remember what she wanted to drink.

"Uh, let's go with a grande pumpkin-spiced latte."

He hovered the tip of a black permanent marker over the white cup he was holding up. "Name?"

"Sarah." She swiped her credit card and stepped aside to wait at the other end of the bar for her drink. She glanced back at Patrick, but he was still working on his lesson plans.

The air in the coffee shop smelled heavenly: a blend of coffee, spices, and sugary treats. A female barista, who judging by her perkiness must have been at the beginning of her shift, pushed Sarah's drink order over the counter to her. With the warm cup in hand, she walked back to Patrick's table and slid into the chair she'd hung her jacket on.

Patrick looked up and smiled. "That didn't take too long."

"It felt like a long time," she said, although in all honesty, the time had flown by because she'd been daydreaming for most of it. All around them, people were chattering, and she had to lean in close to hear him. "It looked like you were working on something over here."

"I was." He flipped a couple pages back in his notebook. "I'm glad we had a chance to meet up today. I wanted to run some of my plans by you for incorporating drama into my classroom this year."

"Sure." She took a sip of her drink, promptly burning her tongue. To cool the coffee down, she removed the lid and set it on a brown paper napkin on the table. "What do you have planned? I've been working on some ideas for my class too."

"Well," he said. "I'm thinking of having my class vote on a book to read and then have them dissect it. Once they've identified all of the important elements of the story, I'll have them create a simple play, using a three-act structure."

She stared at him. Why hadn't she thought of that? "That's a fantastic idea. I think they'll love it."

He flushed. "Thanks. I'm sure it will be a lot of work, but I'm feeling like my lesson plans have become stagnant over the years."

She nodded. "I know what you mean. I've only been at Candle Beach Elementary for a few years, but I don't want to do the same thing every year. I'd like to shake up my lesson plans a little."

"What did you have in mind?" he asked, taking a slug of what must now be lukewarm coffee.

"My kids are a little younger than yours, so I think I'm going to have them create their own play and perform it, rather than base it off a book. I think they'll like it." She stopped, thinking about her class. There were a few shyer kids in the class and she didn't know how they'd react to performing in front of their classmates, but she figured she'd help them through it. Maybe some of them would even discover a love for theater. She hadn't attended a theatrical play until high school and she'd often wished she'd been introduced to theater at a younger age.

"Sounds good." He jotted a few things down in his note-book. "I found a good guidebook for drama in the class-room. I can't remember it right now, but I'll send you the name of it."

"Thanks. I'd like that." She sipped her coffee, which

thankfully now was cool enough to drink without pain. The pumpkin-spiced latte tasted like fall and she made sure to get at least one every year, although she preferred her beloved eggnog latte that reminded her of Christmas. "How's the house remodel going?"

"Slow." He laughed. "With school starting, I've been focused on that and the renovations have been placed on the back burner. Now that I'm more in the swing of things, I'm going to get back to it." He cocked his head to the side. "Did I ever tell you that Parker Gray has a buyer interested in the property?"

She scrunched up her face in thought. "No, I don't think so. I didn't even know you knew Parker. I'm friends with his sister. Actually, she lives above the bookstore where I work."

"He mentioned that when I asked him about you." He clamped his mouth shut, but not before causing her to wonder.

"You asked him about me?"

"Oh, I just mentioned to him that I knew a teacher up in Candle Beach and he said he knew you."

"Ah." She didn't push it any further. "Do you have any plans for Halloween?"

He laughed. "I'm not that into Halloween, but I'll probably dress up as a vampire again this year. My students get a kick out of seeing me in costume."

She grinned. "I bet. I usually play it safe with a witch costume, but I'm more of a Christmas person."

"Not into skeletons and pumpkins?"

"Nah. Although I do enjoy the Fall Harvest Festival at the high school."

"I've never been."

"It's fun. There's bobbing for apples, costume contests, games for the little kids, and other stuff." She shrugged. "I've been going since I was a small child, and now that I teach here, I like seeing the kids in my class participate."

"I'll have to add it to my schedule." He smiled warmly at her, making her core temperature rise.

"Your fiancée must get tired of going to all the school events." Sarah paused. "Or do you not make her go to them? They must get boring after a while."

"My fiancée?" He gave her a puzzled look. "Nina's been gone since last spring."

"Gone?" Her heart beat faster. Did he mean what she thought he meant? Was he single?

He sighed. "Yeah. We parted ways. She needed to find herself or something."

"Oh." A mixture of emotions swirled up inside of her. His fiancée's departure must have been traumatic for him. "I'm sorry. I know the two of you were together for a long time."

"Yeah. We were." Pain crossed his face, but he forced a smile. "It's okay. I'm pretty much over it now."

She scanned his face. It obviously hurt to talk about Nina. But was he ready to date again? A sickening feeling hit her. If his fiancée was gone and he was over her, when he'd offered to fix Sarah up with Derek, he'd subtly told her that he had no interest in her as a woman. So that left them right back where she'd thought, squarely in the friend zone, although now it hurt even worse because she knew he wasn't interested in her in the slightest.

She blinked back tears, then pushed her chair back and stood. "I'd probably better get going. I've got some papers to grade before tomorrow."

"Oh," he said with surprise. "I thought we'd talk a little longer." He chuckled self-consciously. "I don't get much adult conversation time."

"I know the feeling," she said, without thinking. Part of her wanted to stay, to spend more time with Patrick, but the other part of her wanted to get as far away from him as possible so she could deal with the news that he was no longer engaged. How was she going to get over these feelings now?

Inspiration struck. "You know, a friend of mine was just saying she could use more adult conversation. She's a guidance counselor at the middle school and, while she loves her job, she gets tired of the angsty teenagers."

"Are you trying to do some matchmaking?" He laughed. "I guess I deserve that after I fixed you up with my friend. By the way, how did that go?"

She took a deep breath and pasted a smile on her face. "It went well. Derek's a great guy." She hated lying to him, but she needed the protection it gave her.

"Great, great." She felt his eyes search her face and fought the urge to be honest with him. "I guess I could go out on a blind date."

"Fantastic," she said brightly. "I'll let Maura know that you're up for it and give her your phone number."

"I look forward to hearing from her," he said.

She eyed him. "This is kind of fun, right? Fixing each other up with friends?"

"We should call this our matchmaking pact," he quipped.

"Yes. Maybe we should write a song about it and perform it for our classes." She felt her spirits rise as they bantered back and forth. Even if there was no chance of a romantic relationship with him, she was happy to call him a friend.

His eyes danced. "I can see it now. Although our school principals might not be so fond of the concept."

"Maybe not." She couldn't help but laugh at the thought of the stodgy assistant principal's face if he knew what they were joking about. Hopefully their arrangement wouldn't land them in hot water. She stood there awkwardly for a moment, then said, "Well, I'd better go. Good luck with Maura."

"You too."

She turned and left, pushing the door open and walking out into the cold October afternoon. When she'd agreed to meet with Patrick for coffee, she'd resolved not to waste any energy being attracted to him because he was involved with someone else. Now that she knew he wasn't, there was a glimmer of hope that she couldn't quite stamp out, even though she knew it wasn't realistic. Fixing him up with Maura had been a stroke of genius though, and if they hit it off, surely this feeling would go away.

8

*P*atrick drove slowly through the streets of Candle Beach, looking for the address he'd written on a yellow Post-It note. In the middle of October, the skies were dark at this time of night and the streetlights barely provided enough light to see the house numbers.

Finally, he found the right place. It was a small blue Cape Cod style home with red trim and window boxes that held the remains of summer flowers. The yard was neatly manicured and the house itself appeared to have been recently painted. At least in the dark, it was a beautiful specimen of early 1920s architecture. He'd be proud to own a house as nicely maintained as this one.

A few days after they met for coffee, Sarah had come through on her promise to give her friend Maura his phone number. Maura had called him, and they'd arranged for him to pick her up at her house for a dinner date. He still wasn't sure how he felt about going out on a blind date, but he had to get back into the dating world – Nina had been gone for over six months. It could be worse – at least this was a friend of a friend and not some woman he'd met at a bar and knew nothing about. Sarah had vouched for Maura, so she couldn't be that bad.

He'd seen the look of surprise on Sarah's face when he told her that he and Nina had broken up. How had she not known that already? Thinking back though, they hadn't seen each other since last summer, and when they met at the class this past summer, telling her about Nina leaving may not have been at the forefront of his mind since the breakup was months in the past.

He'd like to think that his engagement was the reason Sarah hadn't expressed any interest in him, but even after she knew that Nina had left, she'd still offered to fix him up with her friend. And she and Derek must have hit it off if she was still dating him weeks after their first date, so he'd missed any chance he had with her.

He pushed those thoughts out of his head and, with his palms sweating, rapped sharply on the front door of Maura's house. He'd made reservations for dinner at the Seaside Grille on Main Street. When he and Parker had gone out for beer and wings at the local pub, Parker had mentioned that it was the fanciest restaurant in town and how much Gretchen loved it. He hoped the date would go well, because he didn't know if he could take any more rejection.

A woman answered the door wearing a sleeveless blue dress that showed off her long, shapely legs. Glossy dark hair swung around her shoulders, catching the light streaming from inside the house. Sarah hadn't been talking her up untruthfully. This woman was gorgeous.

She beamed at him. "Patrick?"

He nodded. He liked the way she smiled. But her smile didn't light up her face the way Sarah's did when she was happy about something. *Get it together, Patrick. Sarah isn't interested in you.*

He held out his hand. "Hi. Nice to meet you."

"Hi. I'm Maura. But of course, you know that since you came to my house." She laughed. "It's nice to meet you too, but this is really awkward."

"No kidding." The ice had been broken between them and something about her made him feel comfortable anyway. "I guess this is how Sarah must have felt when I fixed her up with my friend. That seems to have worked out though, so maybe we'll have the same luck." He instantly regretted what he'd said. She must think he sounded like an idiot.

She looked at him sharply, but didn't comment. Instead, she jutted her thumb backward toward the living room. "Let me grab my purse and I'll be all ready to go." She disappeared for a moment, then reappeared with a small black leather purse hanging over her shoulder. She grabbed her coat off of a hook by the door. "How do you feel about walking to town? It's such a nice day."

"Sure," Patrick said. "I wouldn't mind a walk."

She locked the door of her cottage behind them and they walked together down the porch steps to the sidewalk. She breathed deeply. "I love the smell of the sea here."

"Me too." He grinned. This was actually going quite well, or at least as well as possible with thoughts of Sarah lingering in his mind. "Are you not from this area either?"

"No, I'm a transplant from California. I have a cousin who lives in town and I came up to visit her one time and decided to never leave. Luckily, a job at the middle school had just come open, so it was perfect timing. You?" She turned her head up to him.

"I'm from Kansas, but this is where I found a job after college." He gazed down the street toward the restaurant. "I always wonder what it's like to be like Sarah and live in your hometown. She seems to love living here and being near her family. I envy that. Even if I was back in Kansas, I don't know that I'd want to live in the town where I grew up." His parents still lived in the sleepy farming town where he'd attended high school, but it had always felt too confining and landlocked to him.

"I've always wondered too." He felt her eyes on him. "Do you know Sarah well?"

Well? He wouldn't say that, but he'd like to know everything about her. He halted in the middle of the sidewalk and Maura bumped into him. Where had that thought come from? He was on a date with someone else. He needed to focus on his date and not be thinking about another woman.

"Sorry, what did you say?" he asked.

She shot him an odd look. "I was asking how well you know Sarah. She didn't say how long you'd known each other."

"We met last year at a summer continuing education class." Images of them laughing together during and after class spread through his mind. Seriously, he needed to get her out of his head. He walked faster, desperate to have the physical activity distract him.

"Hey," Maura said as she ran up to him, puffing slightly in the frigid air. "I thought you said we were having dinner at the Seaside Grille."

He stopped. "We are, why?"

She pointed up the hill. "Because you passed it half a block ago. You're acting like you're in a speed-walking competition instead of trying to find it."

"I did?" He looked up the street. She was right. "Oh. I'm not very familiar with Candle Beach." He started walking back up the hill, hoping she'd believe his feeble excuse.

She gave him another funny look as she caught up to him. "You sped right past the outside tables and the huge sign with the name of the restaurant on it."

With a sinking feeling, he forced himself to focus. People were already eating on the outside patio and the blue umbrellas flew like bright flags over it all. Real heart lamps lit up the space. How had he missed that?

She put her hand on his arm, forcing him to stop. "What's going on?"

"What do you mean?" He pulled his arm away and fidgeted with his hands in his coat pockets.

She tilted her head to the side, assessing him. "Did you really want to go out with me, or did Sarah make you do it?"

"What? No, of course not. I agreed to this date."

"Well, then what's wrong? I don't know you, but I can tell that something is distracting you. What's going on?"

"Nothing." He kicked a stray pebble off of the sidewalk. "Maybe it's just been a long day for me and I'm not good company."

"If you'd rather, we can just go home." She scanned his face. "No hard feelings."

"No," he said sharply. "I want to go on this date." She stepped back, and he winced at the tone of his voice. She had every right to be wary of him. It didn't matter if he had feelings for Sarah, he was on a date with someone else. From somewhere within the exterior patio area of the Seaside Grille came the telltale sound of glass hitting the ground. He wasn't the only one having a bad evening.

She narrowed her eyes at him. "Look, I'm a guidance counselor at a middle school. I know when something is bothering someone. And don't try to hide it from me, I deal with tweens and early teens. Lying comes second nature to them."

He started to protest, then stopped. What was he supposed to tell her? That he was hung up on her friend? Before he knew it, he'd blurted out that very thing.

"Oh," Maura said in a small voice. His stomach twisted. He'd never meant to hurt her. She was a nice woman and she didn't deserve to have her night ruined by her blind date professing his love for another woman.

Surprisingly though, she brightened quickly. "Does Sarah know that you feel this way?"

"No!" he said loudly. Several patrons at the nearby patio tables stopped eating and stared at him. He lowered his voice. "She's made it pretty clear that she's not interested in me. Please don't say anything to her."

She sighed. "I won't, but I think you should be honest with her. I'm sure she'd like to know because, um…" She stopped. "I mean, what if it doesn't work out between her and that other guy?"

He looked up, suddenly hopeful. "Is it not working out?"

She sighed, and her eyes were troubled. "I don't know. Like I said, you should talk directly to her." She glanced behind her at the front door of the restaurant. "Now what? Should we call it a night?"

His stomach grumbled, and she laughed.

He grinned. "Well, I'm obviously still hungry. Do you want to still have dinner together? As friends," he said quickly. "I'm apparently not in the right state of mind to be dating right now."

She smiled at him and held out her hand to shake with him. "Friends. Now, let's go eat. I'm starving too. I've been checking out their menu all day, trying to decide what to get and I have my heart set on some surf and turf."

"Well then, by all means, let's go. I'm pretty sure I owe you dinner after how I've behaved."

She rested her hand on his arm and smiled up at him. "Don't even worry about how you've behaved. I can't be mad that you have feelings for my best friend. She's a great girl." She grinned widely. "But I do intend to get a nice dinner out of this for keeping my silence."

He laughed. "Deal."

They walked together into the restaurant and had a lovely dinner – surf and turf, which he paid for. When they finished their last bites of buttery steak and shrimp, he tried to talk her into dessert with hopes of plying her for more information about Sarah, but she declined his invitation.

After he walked her home and said goodbye, he left his car parked near her house and returned to the downtown area to tour Main Street for a while longer, enjoying the clear evening. Now that most of the tourists were gone, it wasn't as lively as it had been when he'd come here with Parker, but he liked it this way too. He could see why Sarah was so enchanted by her hometown. There was something calming about walking down the tree-lined streets with the sound of the ocean roaring in the background. An evening fog had rolled in and he stopped to breathe in the dense, salty air.

He still felt bad about unintentionally deceiving Maura, but he was grateful for the gracious way she'd handled things. Although she'd given him hope that Sarah and Derek might part ways, Sarah herself had told him that things were going well between them and he didn't want to do anything to jeopardize that. Hopefully Maura wouldn't say anything to Sarah about his feelings for her until he'd figured out what to do.

9

Sarah couldn't get past her desire to see Patrick, so she figured the best medicine would be to see him and be forced to realize that he only saw her as a friend. The idea of buying a house had been weighing heavily on her mind and she'd enlisted the help of her friend Gretchen, a local real estate agent, to help her see what was available in her price range. She'd called Patrick to see if he would go with her to look at houses since he knew more about them than anyone else she knew. Besides, if it turned out that the only thing she could afford was a fixer-upper, it would be nice to have him with her to provide cost estimates to get things in working order.

When the Saturday morning that she'd arranged to meet Gretchen arrived, she found herself staring at her reflection in the mirror. She'd tried her best to do something with her wavy, shoulder-length hair that was somewhere in between brown and dishwater-blonde, but it refused to fall into neat layers like Maura's hair. Grey-green eyes full of anxiety stared back at her.

From the other side of the room, a squeaking noise tore

her away from her worries. Chuck, her grey and brown hamster, was happily racing to nowhere on the wheel in his cage. She couldn't help but laugh at the earnest expression on his face. Someday, maybe when she had her own place, she'd have a dog but, for now, Chuck was a good roommate.

She took a deep breath and turned back to the mirror, smoothing the soft fabric of her charcoal-gray sweater dress over her hips. Why was she so worried anyway? If the house hunting didn't work out, she'd re-evaluate her desire to own her own home. Although, as much as she'd tried to limit her expectations, she'd secretly be devastated if she couldn't find anything decent that she could afford. And as for Patrick, well, if her plan to see him and get over him didn't work out, she'd figure that out later.

Gretchen had given her a list of available properties in the area and she'd decided to tour everything within her price range that was also within walking distance to the elementary school. They were scheduled to see the first one in ten minutes, so she slid her feet into the tall black boots that she wore for teaching because they were comfortable enough to stand in for hours, and threw on her coat before exiting the apartment.

The first house Gretchen wanted her to see was only a few blocks away – a pretty white Craftsman house with a wide front porch and a cheery yellow door. The garden had seen better days, but then again, it was the middle of October and nothing around there looked at its finest in the gloomy weather. Gretchen was sitting on the porch steps, waiting for her. Patrick had already arrived as well and was circling the exterior of the house. He bent down to examine the foundation, running his hands over a crack in it, then inspected the side of the porch.

Then he noticed she'd arrived and walked over to her.

"Hey," he said, giving her a quick hug that sent shivers all the way down to her boot-encased toes. She stiffened and pulled back, but he didn't seem to notice. "How's it going?"

"Good." She bit her lip. Should she ask him about his date with Maura? She mentally debated with herself and finally spat it out. "How did your date with Maura go? I haven't had a chance to talk with her since then."

He looked down and toed the ground, then looked up, smiling. "It went well. We had a nice time together."

"Oh." Her heart twinged and she looked away. "That's great. I'm glad it worked out for the two of you."

He nodded but didn't respond to her comment verbally.

She pointed at the porch. "Is everything okay with the foundation?"

"It looks good to me. I would expect to see a few cracks in the foundation of a house of this age, but there was nothing too serious. Although when you get to the stage of having a house inspected, they'll be able to look at it in more detail."

She nodded, her anxiety returning. There were so many things to remember about the home-buying process. It was all a little overwhelming.

Gretchen cleared her throat. "So, this is a three-bedroom, one-bath house that was built in the early 1900s."

"Great." Sarah ran her eyes over the front of the house. A thrill ran through her. This was really happening. She wasn't sure yet how many bedrooms she needed, although she wanted at least two, but she wouldn't object to more. As Maura had said, her craft items needed room to spread out.

Gretchen climbed the steps and unlocked the front door. The lock stuck, and she had to jiggle it, but then the handle turned easily, and the door swung open. They entered a living room with thick brown carpet and a fireplace with the original unpainted bricks and mantel. It was small, but plenty big enough for her.

Gretchen led them down a small hallway to the back of the house where they found a kitchen with torn vinyl flooring, oak cabinets and laminate counter tops.

"As you can see, the kitchen was last remodeled in the mid-eighties, so it's not in the best of shape cosmetically, but the good news is that they renovated all of the wiring and plumbing at the same time. Some of the houses in this area still have knob and tube wiring that should be replaced for safety."

"Is that type of thing expensive?" Sarah definitely didn't want to have an unsafe home but rewiring a house couldn't be cheap.

"Yep. They can be," Gretchen said. "That's definitely a plus for this property versus some others we may see." She gestured to a door. "This leads out to the backyard. Do you want to see it now, or later?"

Sarah glanced at Patrick and he shrugged. "Now is good," she said.

The sheer curtain over the window in the door fluttered as Gretchen pushed the door open. The backyard was a normal size for the city and, like the front yard, was badly in need of some landscaping. However, there was a nice surprise in the corner of the yard – a built-in firepit and patio.

"I love it," she said softly. Visions of backyard barbecues with all of her friends flowed through her mind. Maybe someday there would be little kids here, if she was ever fortunate enough to find the right person to settle down with. There was just enough room for a small swing set toward the other side of the yard.

She shivered as a cool breeze swept across the yard.

"Let's see the rest of the house." Gretchen led them back into the kitchen and then into a dining room with a built-in cabinet with leaded glass door panes.

Patrick crossed over to it immediately to inspect it further. "This is a beautiful piece of craftsmanship." He pulled a drawer open and it slid easily. "They've added some slides to this to help with functionality, but otherwise it's original to the house."

Sarah pulled a drawer open as well, loving how the coolness of the cut glass knobs felt beneath her fingertips. When she'd talked to Gretchen about houses, she hadn't known exactly what she wanted, but now she knew that having a house with history was important to her.

"Ready to go upstairs?" Gretchen pointed at a back staircase. "We can see the main floor bathroom when we come back down."

"Sure," Sarah said as she followed Gretchen up the stairs.

The three bedrooms upstairs were in decent condition, as was the bathroom downstairs, with its wide subway tiles and vintage standing sink and claw-foot bathtub.

Soon they were standing outside of the house, staring up at it as they had when they first arrived.

Sarah glanced at Patrick's face. It was poker straight and she couldn't tell what he was thinking.

He walked closer to the house with his hands in his pockets, gazing up at it.

"What do you think?" Her stomach churned. There were other houses to see, but she wasn't sure any of them would top this one. If there was something major wrong with it, she'd be crushed.

His eyes met hers and his face erupted in a smile. "For the price point, I think it's in great condition. There's a few minor things that I see that need to be fixed, but from a quick walk-through of the house, the bones of it appear to be good."

She breathed a sigh of relief. "But you don't think there's anything that would be too costly to fix?"

He shrugged. "I mean, you never know until you get a formal inspection, but I'm not seeing anything that's triggering any alarms for me."

"Is having a second bathroom important to you?" Gretchen asked. "Some of my clients are adamant about the need for more than one bathroom."

Sarah shrugged. "It's just me, so I can't see that I'd need more than one."

"I think you could put one in upstairs next to the landing if you'd like," Patrick said, staring at the house as if trying to remember the layout. "It would be on top of the other bathroom, so the plumbing shouldn't be too tricky."

She nodded. "Good to know." If she ever had more people living there with her, having an extra bathroom might be nice. Good thing Patrick had agreed to come see houses with her or she'd never have known adding a second bath would be possible.

Gretchen looked from Patrick to Sarah. "Do you still want to see the other houses?"

"Yes," Sarah said. Although this particular house spoke to her, she wanted to make sure she wasn't experiencing some weird effect from it being the first and only house she'd toured.

"Okay, let's go then." Gretchen locked the front door and placed the key in the lockbox, then guided them a few blocks over to the next house.

This house was in a similar style to the first, but much care had been given to the exterior of the house. It had been painted navy-blue with a red door and accents, and gave her a cheery feeling, even in the dullness of winter.

"So this one is a little smaller, a two-bedroom with one bath. However, it's priced quite a bit lower than the first." Gretchen let them into the house.

The interior was just as nice as the exterior and had obviously been remodeled in the last five years or so. The kitchen had been renovated, although the fixtures weren't high-end. Although a fancy kitchen would have been nice, Sarah would be happy with anything with more space than the kitchen in her rental. Like the other house, there was a door leading outside from the kitchen.

Sarah walked over to it, turning the knob, not sure what she'd find. When she saw the backyard, she felt a twinge of sadness. It was much smaller than the other house's backyard and didn't have room for a playset, much less for a firepit. It was big enough for a compact table and chairs and a vegetable garden, but maybe that was all she needed. Still though, it didn't give her the same feeling as the first house.

The rest of the house was unremarkable, and they found themselves standing outside in a few minutes.

"What did you think?" Gretchen eyed Sarah.

Sarah hesitated.

"You didn't like it as much as the first one, did you?" Gretchen asked.

She sighed. "No." Even though this one was cheaper, it didn't have as much potential as the house they'd seen earlier.

"I think the first one had more going for it," Patrick said. "The house itself was bigger and so was the yard."

Gretchen looked at Sarah. "Do you want to put an offer in on the first house or do you want to see the other houses on the list?"

"I don't know. I did love that first one." Sarah bit her lip. She hadn't expected to find something she loved so quickly. "How fast do you think it will go?"

Gretchen checked the listing that she'd printed out and attached to her clipboard. "You never know, but I would think it will sell fairly fast. It's a new listing and while it's not the prettiest house on the block, it's a good size and condition for the price."

Sarah took a deep breath, her heart hammering. "Okay. I'll do it."

Gretchen gave her a small hug. "I know it's scary. It's probably the biggest purchase you'll ever make, but I think if we can get you this house, you'll love it."

Sarah nodded. Was anyone ever sure they were making the right decision when it came to buying a house? She took another deep breath and smiled at Gretchen.

Gretchen smiled back. "Let's go back to my office and we can write up an offer, okay?" She glanced at Patrick. "Did you want to come too?"

He looked at Sarah and then quickly away, as if he couldn't wait to get away from her. "No, I'd probably be a third wheel for that. I think I'll head back to Haven Shores – I've got some things I need to do today. Sarah, I'm glad you found something you like. Let me know if there's anything else I can do to help you."

"I will. Thank you." Sarah stuck her hands in her coat pockets and turned her attention back to the house to take her mind off of him.

"It was nice to meet you, Patrick," Gretchen said warmly. "And if you decide to sell the house you're working on, I've got some clients that are looking for something like it."

He laughed. "Are you trying to snag my house out from under Parker?"

She reddened, then laughed. "You got me. Parker and I have a friendly competition going of who can sell the most houses this year. I'm a few behind him. But seriously, I have clients that might be interested."

He gave her a smile. "I'll keep that in mind." He eyed Sarah again. "But I'd better get going. Thanks for letting me tag along today." He hurried out of there, probably racing back for a date with Maura.

Sarah felt ill thinking of him dating Maura. She hadn't talked to her friend lately because school had been busy for both of them, but she assumed that Maura and Patrick would have hit it off on their date.

Apparently her plan to desensitize herself from Patrick hadn't worked as well as she'd hoped. It didn't really matter though. If she got this house, she wouldn't have much time for dating between renovating the property and her teaching job. Things may not have been going the way she'd like for this stage in her life, but she felt as though she was making strides.

Gretchen smiled at her. "Well, are you ready?"

Sarah looked at her friend. She trusted Gretchen's judgment and Patrick had given his blessing on this house as well. It was time to throw caution to the wind and take a leap of faith. "You know, I think I am."

10

*S*arah didn't see Patrick for another two weeks, in which time she managed to convince herself that any romantic feelings she'd had for him had passed. Gretchen had called to tell her that the owners of the house had accepted her offer, and she'd been busy getting everything together for her mortgage application.

At school, her fourth graders were getting more and more excited about Halloween, and the Fall Harvest Festival had finally arrived to usher in the holiday season. As she'd told Patrick, she looked forward to going to it every year.

This year she didn't dress up for the festival, although some of her students used it as an excuse to wear their new costumes prior to Halloween. She'd asked several of her friends if they'd like to go with her, but none of them had been available, so she'd decided to go alone. It wasn't that bad though – there was plenty to do and she busied herself with participating in the games and talking with her students and their parents.

Although it could be seen as childish, one of her favorite events at the festival was the donut-eating contest. In the contest, mini powdered-sugar donuts were hung from strings and each contestant had to eat their donut faster than the person across from them. When the round in front of her was complete, she moved into her place along the line of donuts while chatting with one of her students, who was next to her in line.

The announcer warned them that the race was about to begin, and she turned her attention to the donut in front of her – and the man on the other side of the donut. She had to do a double-take when she realized who it was.

"Patrick?" The last time she'd seen him was when they'd gone house hunting together and she hadn't heard from him again. She'd told him she always went to the Fall Harvest Festival, so if he was trying to avoid her now, he wasn't doing a very good job of it.

He gave her a devilish grin. "I didn't want to interrupt you while you were talking with that kid, but I plan to beat you in this competition." He waggled his eyebrows at her.

She narrowed her eyes at him, trying to conceal laughter of her own. A sense of wistfulness rushed through her. Patrick's playfulness was one of the reasons why she loved spending time with him. If only she could find someone just like him. She fought to push that thought out of her mind and just enjoy the moment. "You think you can beat me? I've been winning this contest since I was a little kid."

The announcer called out, "Ready, set, go." All around them, people awkwardly tried to eat the donuts dangling in front of them with their hands pressed to their backs.

The donuts were hung low enough that even the littlest of kids could participate, and she and Patrick had to sink down in a duck squat to eat them. She nudged at the donut with her lips, but it kept bouncing off her cheek as she tried to bite into it, sending showers of powdered sugar all over her face. She attempted to come up from underneath it and lost her balance in the extreme crouch, falling forward into Patrick. He reached out to catch her, but he couldn't stop her momentum. Their lips touched as he toppled backward, still holding on to her.

For a moment, she couldn't move. His lips were soft, warm and coated with powdered sugar. All of the feelings she'd struggled to deny cascaded over her and she was helpless in his arms. He held her there for a few seconds longer than necessary, then helped her to standing. Around them, people were cheering. She assumed it was because a winner had been declared until she saw a few of her students staring at her.

"Ms. Rigg was kissing him," they said in excited voices as they pointed to Patrick, who still held her in his arms, steadying her. He looked unperturbed by the pint-sized onlookers, but her legs were as wobbly as a toddler's.

Sarah blushed to the roots of her hair and quickly extracted herself from Patrick's grip, studiously averting her eyes from his face. Then she jogged over to the women's restroom and locked herself in a stall before taking a breath to calm herself.

Her fingers went to her lips, which still tasted of powdered sugar. What had that been? Had they really kissed? She'd accidentally bumped into him, but her feelings for him were no accident. As much as she'd tried to avoid them, they weren't going to go away easily.

She left the stall and stood at the sink, splashing water on her face until her cheeks paled. Great. Now not only had she kissed Patrick, but she'd probably be receiving phone calls from parents asking why she'd been kissing someone in front of their kids.

A group of teenage girls came into the bathroom,

gabbing excitedly about a boy they'd just seen. If only life as an adult were that easy. She left, trying to sneak away from the carnival without anyone seeing her. If she could make it to the exit, she could leave and pretend that the kiss had never happened.

"Wait," someone called out to her. She cringed and froze in place. So much for escaping.

She turned to see Patrick running up to her. He was the last person she wanted to see at the moment. Heat rose up her neck and into her cheeks again. She attempted to compose herself before he reached her.

"I'm really sorry about what happened earlier," she blurted out. "I didn't mean to fall into you...or any of the rest of it. I just lost my balance."

"Don't worry about it." He smiled at her. "I wanted to make sure you were okay though. You ran away so fast."

"I'm fine." She glanced longingly at the exit. This was one of the most embarrassing conversations she'd ever had. She checked his expression to see if he felt the same, but he was staring at something over her shoulder.

His face blanched and she turned to see what was bothering him.

A beautiful woman in her early thirties and a man who was a few years older were walking toward them with an elementary-aged child. Sarah didn't recognize the little girl, but she may have gone to a different elementary than the one where she taught. The woman halted when she saw Patrick.

"Patrick. It's nice to see you." She smiled, but the smile didn't quite reach her eyes.

"Nina." Pain flashed across his face as he eyed the woman.

"This is my fiancé William and his daughter Angela."

She gestured to the man and little girl next to her, who didn't appear to have any clue as to what was going on.

Sarah stared at her. Who was this woman? Then it hit her. This was his ex-fiancée, the woman who'd broken his heart.

"Your fiancé?" Beside her, Patrick sputtered and almost choked on the words.

Sarah had never seen him so rattled and her heart went out to him. It must be killing him to see her engaged to another man so soon after breaking up with him.

Nina looked pointedly at Sarah. "And this is?"

He glanced down at Sarah. "This is..."

She took a deep breath, pasted a smile on her face, and held her hand out to Nina. "I'm Sarah, Patrick's girlfriend."

Nina's red-stained lips formed an O and her gaze darted between the two of them, as if she wasn't sure whether or not to believe Sarah.

Patrick didn't seem to know how to react either. He met Sarah's eyes, questioning her.

She nodded, and he said, "Yes, Sarah is my girlfriend. We've been dating for a few months now." He put his arm around her shoulders and chills ran through her.

"Oh? I'd heard you weren't dating anyone." Nina eyed him with suspicion.

Did she really say that? Had she been keeping tabs on Patrick? It was almost as if she didn't think he should be happy.

Without any thought to the possibility of her students seeing it, Sarah turned to Patrick and reached up to cup the back of his head with her hand, gently tugging him down toward her upturned face. He stared at her in surprise, but then seemed to realize what she was doing and covered her lips with his.

The outside world disappeared, and it was just her and Patrick. His hands were placed tentatively on her back and his touch seared through her jacket. She never wanted the kiss to end.

Nina cleared her throat and a cold wave washed over Sarah, breaking the trance. What had she done? She'd been trying to help Patrick when he was in distress, but she'd kissed the man her friend was dating – and she was the one who'd brought them together in the first place. She was the worst friend ever.

Patrick put his arm around her again, pulling her close. Sarah fought to catch her breath, afraid that if she said anything, it would come out as a squeak. She pressed her lips together and a burst of powdered sugar hit her tongue, but its sweetness made her mood even more sour.

Nina stared at them, then said to her fiancé, "We'd better go. Angi's been wanting to do the cake walk." She turned away, then said to Patrick over her shoulder, "Nice seeing you again."

He nodded and gave her a cool wave as she walked away.

Sarah turned to him, her blood chilled. Any lasting effect from their passionate kiss had worn off. Her words came out in a rush. "I'm so sorry for kissing you like that. I don't know what I was thinking."

He hesitated for a moment, as if choosing his words carefully. "Don't worry about it. You helped me out of a tight spot." He shook his head. "I can't believe she's already engaged to someone else." He looked her in the eyes. "I don't have feelings for her anymore or any hopes that we'd ever get back together, but there are a lot of memories there. It feels like she tossed them away without any regard. And he has a kid – when we were together, she was never keen on having a kid in the future."

"I get that," Sarah said slowly, still trying to understand what had just happened. "By approaching you, she was almost flaunting her new relationship in your face. Still, it was wrong of me to do that."

His eyes searched her face and she bit her lip to keep from crying. She'd really screwed up. "Okay, then let's forget it ever happened." He smiled at her.

Was it even possible to forget they'd kissed – twice? Somehow, she didn't think so, but she found herself agreeing with him. She didn't want him gone from her life, but things between them kept getting worse instead of better.

"Are we good?" he asked. "I don't want things to be awkward between us. I value your friendship."

There it was again. Friendship. She was completely in the friend zone in his mind – not that she'd expected anything different.

"Of course," she said with forced cheer in her voice. All she wanted to do was to get out of there before any sense of bravado lapsed. She eyed the exit. It was so close. If she left immediately though, it might look weird.

She fought for something to say to him, and then it hit her – the house. "I got the house." Her spirits lifted.

His face lit up. "You did? That's wonderful. Are you excited?" He moved toward her as if he was going to give her a hug, but she backed away, effectively putting a wall between them. He dropped his arms and grinned at her instead. "I'm really happy for you, Sarah. I think you'll like being a homeowner."

"I hope so." She twisted the hem of her sweater sleeve. "I'm still nervous about it."

"Eh, that's normal. You'll get used to it. Do you know when you can move in?"

"They think it should go through in early December." She could already smell the Christmas cookies she'd make in the big kitchen and the lights she'd hang from the eaves of the house.

"Just in time for Christmas. It's your favorite holiday, right?"

"It is." She looked at him in amazement. How had he remembered that? "I'll probably hold off on remodeling until after then, but I'd like to get the kitchen redone in the next few months. I'm feeling a little out of my depth though. There are so many choices for the things in the kitchen."

"Well, if you need anything, give me a call." He checked his watch. "I need to head home, but I'll see you sometime soon, okay?"

"Yep." She watched him saunter away, still chiding herself over kissing him. Although he hadn't appeared to hate the kiss, it obviously hadn't been as mind-blowing to him as it had been for her.

11
----

*P*atrick stared at the railing in front of him and groaned. He'd been sanding the same patch of wood for the last ten minutes and his efforts had worn a ragged patch in the finish. He couldn't get Sarah or the kiss they'd shared at the Fall Harvest Festival out of his mind. When she'd fallen into him during the mini-donut-eating contest, he hadn't known what to say. So many emotions had shot through him as their lips touched for the briefest of moments.

When he'd found her after their accidental kiss, she'd been so upset by it that he'd told her it was no big deal – but it was to him. In that kiss he'd felt a connection with her, and the bond became even stronger when she kissed him later. The second kiss may have been fake to her, but he knew the instant that Sarah's lips touched his that he no longer had feelings for Nina or hopes that she'd come back to him. Sarah was all he could think about.

He was sure now that he was ready to start a new life, hopefully with Sarah. The problem was, he didn't know if she was still dating Derek. There was no way that he could horn in on their relationship since he'd set them up in the first place.

On a whim, he called Derek on the phone.

"Hey, man," he said when Derek answered.

"Hey, Patrick. What's up buddy?"

"Not much. Just been finishing up this house and I realized I hadn't talked to you in a while." Patrick paced the hardwood floors in the kitchen, staring at the refinished oak planks as he walked.

"Yeah, it has been a while. I think the last time we talked was when you set me up with a friend of yours – Sarah, was it?"

Hope crept into Patrick's chest. Derek couldn't even remember Sarah's name. How was that even possible? But it did mean that they couldn't be dating.

"How did that work out with her, anyway?" Patrick forced himself to stop pacing and sat down on the stairs.

Derek was silent, as if straining to remember. Finally, he said, "You know, we just weren't very compatible. We barely made it through the first date."

"Oh, that's too bad. I was really hoping the two of you would hit it off." Patrick hoped he had put enough sympathy in his voice, although his entire being was shouting "Yes!"

"Yeah. No biggie though. I'm actually dating someone now that I met at the gym," Derek said. "Hey, do you want to get together for a beer sometime and catch up?"

"Yeah, that'd be great. Text me the day and time and I'll be there." Patrick's heart pounded, his mind reeling at the revelation that Sarah might be single.

"Okay, bud. Talk to you later."

"You too." Patrick set his phone down on the counter. Sarah might not be with Derek, but was she involved with anyone else? He doubted that a beautiful, smart woman like her would be single for long. But now that he knew he had a shot at a future with her, he had to give it a try. After their last interaction though, would things be awkward? He couldn't just show up at her front door and proclaim his undying affection for her. He needed to test the waters first to see if his feelings were reciprocated.

What could he use as an excuse to visit her? His eyes roamed around the kitchen. He'd finished the remodel in there, but he still had all of the catalogs and some samples he'd used to choose the building materials for the project. Sarah had mentioned being a little intimidated by the prospect of a kitchen remodel. Bringing her the samples would be a perfect excuse for a visit. Even if he struck out with her in the romance department, he'd at least be helping her.

First though, where did she live? Although he'd seen her new house, he'd never been to her current house before. An idea popped into his head and he rummaged around in the closet under the stairs where he'd stashed the Christmas cards he'd received last year. Nina had chided him about keeping so much old mail, but he always had good intentions of sending out cards of his own and would need the addresses. He dug through the box. Aha. He triumphantly held up the envelope with Sarah's return address printed neatly in the corner.

He grabbed the building material samples and jumped in his car, driving straight to her house in Candle Beach. When he reached her door, the sounds of her singing along to Jingle Bell Rock reverberated through the door.

A grin spread across his face. She'd been serious when she said she loved Christmas. It was only late October and he hadn't even decorated for Halloween yet. Even the department stores waited until after Thanksgiving to start blasting Christmas music.

He rapped on the door, loud enough to be heard over the music. The song shut off abruptly. A minute later, the door swung open. He sucked in his breath.

Sarah stood in the entry, wearing a red sweater and jeans, with a thin gold chain around her neck. Her hair was piled high in a messy bun atop her head, with tendrils escaping from it and cascading down her flushed cheeks. She was beautiful, although he was sure she'd never believe it if he told her so. The scent of something savory and delicious wafted out of the apartment.

With puzzlement, she turned her head up to scan his face. "Patrick? What are you doing here? We didn't have plans, did we?"

He froze. Was it weird for him to have come here unannounced? He awkwardly held up the armful of catalogs and samples. "I thought these might be useful when you decide to remodel the kitchen in your new house."

Her eyes lit up. "Are those tile samples?"

He nodded, and she grabbed a few of them from him. "These are lovely. Did you use them in your kitchen?"

He breathed a sigh of relief. His plan was working. Maybe he'd have a chance to tell her how he felt about her after all.

"I used the brighter, smaller tiles as a backsplash behind the stove and then used the larger subway tiles for the rest of the wall." He shivered, and she seemed to realize that he was still standing outside.

She motioned for him to enter. "Come in, come in. It's freezing out there."

He acquiesced, and she shut the door behind him. "Let's go into the living room. It's warmer in there than the other rooms in this place. I swear it's impossible to regulate the temperature in this house. It's either too warm or too cold. I definitely won't miss that when I move."

She perched on the edge of an armchair and set the samples on the coffee table. He placed the catalogs on the table too and sat across from her on the couch, his eyes roving around the room. Sarah had decorated for Christmas already, even though he assumed she'd be in her new place by then. A tree sat in the corner, decked out in a wide variety of ornaments and strings of small colorful lights. She'd set up a whole village of ceramic houses on a coffee table against the window.

When she caught his gaze, her cheeks turned pink. "Yeah, as you can see, I'm a little nutty about the holidays." She shrugged and smiled at him. "What can I say? I've always loved the season."

He grinned back at her. "It's very festive. I bet you'll have fun decorating your new house."

She nodded. "I'm already making plans for it." She gestured to the sample building materials. "Thank you so much for bringing me these. I think they'll really come in handy."

"Of course. I saw them on my kitchen counter and I thought you might be able to use them." She appeared to be genuinely happy to see him and he took a deep breath. "Sarah, there's something I wanted to talk with you about."

A timer pinged. She glanced at him apologetically and popped up from the couch. "Hold that thought. I've got to go check on the pot roast I have in the oven. I'll be right back."

She was making a roast for herself? He got up to see if there was anything he could do to help her in the kitchen. When he walked through the small dining area, he noticed that the table was formally set for two people, with both water and wine glasses. Definitely not a casual dinner for herself. Things weren't looking too good for this being his moment.

He cleared his throat. "I came at a bad time. It looks like you're having company for dinner. I don't want to intrude."

"No, you're fine," she called through the pass-through between the kitchen and the dining nook. "Adam won't be here for a while longer. I'm glad you stopped by. I was beginning to worry that things were awkward between us, you know...after what happened at the harvest festival."

He stared at the floor, happy that she couldn't see his expression. The harvest festival. Yeah, things were definitely awkward between them, because he couldn't stop thinking about her. He glanced at the table setting again. He had to get out of there before her dinner date showed up. Meeting him would make things ten times worse.

"You know, I forgot I was supposed to do something tonight. I'll leave these with you and maybe we can go over them another time."

"Are you sure?" She came out of the kitchen to peer at him, a confused expression on her face. "I thought there was something you needed to tell me."

"Was there? I forgot what it was, but if I remember I'll let you know. I'm sure if it was important, it'll come back to me." A little part of him died inside as he made his way to the door. She followed him, leaning against the open doorframe.

"Well, it was nice seeing you," she said, wrapping her arms across her chest for warmth.

"You too. Feel free to do what you like with the samples. I don't need them any longer." His body was screaming at him to not leave, but he knew he had to get out of there fast if he wanted to avoid meeting her date.

"I'll do that, thank you." She smiled at him, then gently closed the door.

He hurried out to his car. As he was pulling away from the curb, he saw another car coming from behind him. By the time he'd stopped at the stop sign on the corner, a man with bright red hair had exited the car and was approaching Sarah's apartment with a small bouquet of flowers clutched in his hands.

Patrick groaned out loud. Unfortunately, he'd been right. She was having another man over for dinner tonight. He'd missed out on his chance with her after the date with Derek didn't work out. Once again, they were ships passing in the night.

12

The Friday before Thanksgiving, Sarah was counting down the hours until school was over. The elementary school was closed for the week of Thanksgiving, although she still had parent-teacher conferences to do on Monday and Tuesday. With the school break approaching, her students were wired and having difficulty concentrating on any subject.

At the end of the day, she clapped her hands together to get her class's attention. "Alright. I need everyone to gather up their backpacks and then sit at their desks for closing."

The kids bounced out of their seats and into the hallway to grab their belongings, taking twice as long as usual to return. She'd expected that though. The days leading up to school breaks were never terribly productive. When they were settled again, she handed out their reading assignments for the next week and then asked, "What are you all having for Thanksgiving dinner?"

"Corn muffins!" one student shouted.

"Turkey," said another, and her class erupted in cheers as the others echoed him. "I love turkey!"

"Cranberries." The little girl who'd said that had a dreamy expression on her face. "I like the cranberries. They're so pretty and yummy and my mom makes the best cranberry and fruit salad."

Sarah grinned. She loved seeing her students get excited about things. One little boy had remained quiet though. She moved over to his desk.

"Tommy," she said. "What are you looking forward to eating?"

He hesitated. "I don't know. I don't think we're having Thanksgiving this year. Mom said everything costs too much." A tear pooled in the corner of his left eye.

"Oh." His words smacked her in the stomach. She knew that some of her students were from lower-income families, but she hadn't thought about that when she'd asked the class about their Thanksgiving plans. "You know, I bet you're going to have a great holiday anyway." Her words sounded false, even to her own ears.

"Maybe." He tried to smile. The other kids were staring at him. She had to do something to get their attention off of him. The clock read two minutes to release time. The end of day attendants would be out there already to lead them to their buses, so it wouldn't hurt to dismiss them a bit early.

She held her hands up and waved. "Okay everyone, class dismissed."

"Woohoo!" The kids, including Tommy, rushed out of the classroom.

Sarah sat back down at her desk and stared at her grade book without seeing it. Was there anything she could do for Tommy and his family? There had to be something. She pushed herself to standing and strode down to the principal's office.

She knocked on the door. "Jane?"

Jane Andersen looked up. "Hi, Sarah. Did you need something?"

"Uh, yes. I was wondering if there were any programs in place for getting Thanksgiving meals to some of our students' families. I have a student whose family is in need – Tommy Jensen."

"Well, yes, there are." Jane's face fell. "But the families needed to have signed up for them a few weeks ago. All of the meals that have been donated have already been allocated."

"Oh." If only she'd known earlier. "Thanks anyway. Have a nice break."

"You too." Jane went back to what she'd been working on and Sarah left.

On the way home, Sarah couldn't help but dwell on Tommy's situation. She didn't have much extra money, especially with the new house, but she could probably afford to buy them something to make their holidays special. It was a small town and she knew where many of her students lived, including Tommy. It would be a simple matter to drop off a turkey and some fixings for them.

With the holidays fast approaching, Sarah hadn't seen much of her group of friends in Candle Beach. So, when Dahlia asked that everyone meet her for happy hour at Off the Vine, the local wine bar, Sarah was excited to join them. Seeing Tommy so sad about Thanksgiving earlier in the day had darkened her mood and she hoped an evening with her friends would be exactly what she needed.

When she arrived at the wine bar at five o'clock that night, the sky was dark, and the wine bar was almost full.

Luckily, Dahlia had claimed the corner booth where they could all fit without feeling squished against each other.

Sarah walked over to the booth and slid into the seat next to Dahlia.

Charlotte smiled at her from across the table. "I'm glad you could make it tonight."

"Me too." Sarah shook her head. "It's been a long day."

"Are you working at the bookstore tomorrow?" Charlotte asked.

"Yes." Sarah glanced at Dahlia. "We should be busy. I'm already getting parents coming in to buy Christmas presents for their kids."

A satisfied smile crossed Dahlia's face. "This is shaping up to be a great year at the store."

Charlotte scooted out from the booth with her purse in hand. "I'm going to powder my nose. If the waitress comes by, can you please order me a Pinot Grigio?"

Sarah nodded. "Yep, I'll tell her." She turned to Dahlia. "I'm not sure yet what I want to drink, but I've been dreaming about loaded nachos all day. Maybe a margarita would go best with those."

"Ah, a margarita sounds good." Dahlia picked up the drinks menu and flipped through it, then set it back on the table. "But I think I'm more in the mood for a milkshake tonight. I was thinking about Aunt Ruth today when I was working on the window display and wondered what she'd think about the changes I've made to the bookstore." A shadow crossed her face and she shook it off. "Anyway, I saw on the chalkboard that they have banana milkshakes on special tonight. Aunt Ruth always made me banana milkshakes when I'd visit, so it almost seems like a sign from her."

Sarah smiled. "I'm sure she'd think you've done a great job on it."

"I hope so." Dahlia sighed. "I've been putting everything I have into it, but I'm not sure I can continue doing that. That's why I'm so glad you're on board to help with the upcoming Christmas rush."

"Of course. I'm happy to help." Sarah put her hand on top of Dahlia's for a moment. Something was really bothering her. Was this why she'd asked her friends to meet her for happy hour?

"Hey guys, sorry I'm late." Gretchen rushed over to them, her long dark hair flying behind her. "It's been crazy at work. Everyone wants to get into a new house before Christmas."

Sarah grinned. "I know how they feel."

"Oh yeah." Gretchen frowned. "I wanted to talk to you about that."

From her tone of voice, it wasn't something good. An ominous feeling came over Sarah.

"Is there a problem with the house?" She held her breath, not sure she wanted to know. It had seemed too good to be true that she'd found such a great house and the seller had accepted her offer.

"Well, not the house itself. The appraisal was good on it, but the sellers are dragging their feet on making some of the repairs that the bank requires."

Sarah's jaw dropped, and she pushed herself back in the seat, staring at Gretchen. "But they agreed to it."

Gretchen gave her an apologetic look. "I know. This happens sometimes. Sometimes, it can be difficult to get someone in to perform the repairs, so it may not even be their fault."

"But won't that affect my mortgage?"

Gretchen shrugged. "It's pretty common. I'm sure they'll have the repairs done in time for closing. It's annoying, but unfortunately, working with the sellers is just part of the home buying process." She smiled at Sarah, seeming to notice the panicked note in her voice. "Don't worry about it. If it were serious, I'd tell you, okay?"

Sarah took a deep breath. "Okay. Thanks for bearing with me on this. It's such a big purchase and every little thing that goes wrong makes me worry that I'm doing the wrong thing."

"Totally normal," Gretchen said. "Even my clients that have bought several houses go through the same thing. I promise." She reached for the menu. "Have you ordered yet? Maggie called me and said she and Angel were going to be late. There was something going on at the café that they needed to take care of."

"Nope." Dahlia handed Gretchen a menu. "I can't decide what I want. I'm starving, but everything looks good to me and I can't decide."

Charlotte returned to the table. "Did the waitress come by yet?"

"Nope," Sarah said. "You still have time to add your food order on."

"Oh good." Charlotte brightened. "Luke was telling me all about his new barbecue sauce and now I want some barbecue wings."

"Good evening." The twenty-something waitress smiled at them, revealing perfectly straight teeth. "Are you ready to order?"

"We are," Charlotte said. "But there are two more people in our party that will be here soon."

A flicker of annoyance crossed the waitress's face. "Do you want to order now, or later?"

"Now is good," Dahlia said quickly. "They can order when they get here."

They all placed their orders. Dahlia couldn't decide, so she got two appetizers for them to share.

After she left, Charlotte said, "She must be new. She seemed a little flustered."

"Probably. Or maybe she's having an off day. I think little kids are stressful sometimes, but adult customers are probably ten times worse." Sarah turned to Dahlia. "So what's going on? What's the big news?" When she'd seen Dahlia the day before at the bookstore, she hadn't said anything other than to invite her to happy hour.

Dahlia smiled at her mysteriously "I'll tell you when everybody gets here."

Gretchen laughed. "Must be a juicy secret. Ooh, is one of Garrett's books being made into a movie?"

Dahlia just smiled. "Nope. Although he did have a call from his agent recently about movie rights. I'm not telling you anything until Maggie and Angel get here."

"Oh, fine." Charlotte sighed dramatically. "I hate secrets though. I'm way too impatient."

"Seriously?" Dahlia laughed. "I'll tell you as soon as they get here, okay?"

"Okay." Charlotte looked at Sarah. "While we're waiting, I want to hear all about your new house. Where's it at? When do you get to move in?"

"It's only a few blocks from my rental house. I'll still be able to walk to work and to town."

The waitress came by with their drink orders and Sarah licked some salt off the rim of her glass, then sipped from it. She hadn't had much to eat that day and didn't want it to go to her head before she ate.

"That's great," Dahlia said, pouring her milkshake from

93

the silver container it had been mixed in, into a tall glass. "Will you move in before Christmas?" She stuck her straw in the drink and inhaled it for a moment, then peered at Sarah. "Are you sure you'll have time to work at the bookstore with everything going on right now?"

"Definitely," Sarah promised. "I've already started packing." She crossed her fingers under the table. One box of linens packed counted as having started, right? "I close on December second. Well, if everything goes according to plan." She smiled. "If anyone wants to volunteer themselves or their significant others to help me move, I wouldn't say no. I've already roped Adam into it."

"Don't be surprised if the closing date gets pushed out by a little bit, though," Gretchen said. The waitress had brought by their food and she reached for a fry and dipped it in the house special sauce.

Unease rose in Sarah's chest. Gretchen had said that it was normal for the banks to take a while with the mortgage. Had she been hiding the truth?

Gretchen sensed her concern and smiled at her.

"Again, don't worry, it's totally normal. Sometimes the banks take a little bit longer to verify everything. I just want you to be prepared in case closing is extended. But it will probably close on time. I've seen your paperwork. Everything was neat as a pin in there."

Sarah nodded, but worrying about Dahlia and the house had diminished her appetite. Gretchen had helped her go over the mortgage paperwork to make sure that she wasn't forgetting anything. She'd just have to take it one day at a time. Still, Gretchen's comments gave her pause. Buying a house was even more complicated than she had initially thought.

Maggie arrived, with Angel in tow. They removed their winter jackets and crowded into the booth.

"I'm so hungry I could eat a horse," Maggie said.

"You've got to take better care of yourself," Angel scolded her. "Did you even have lunch today?"

"I wasn't hungry earlier." Maggie shrugged. "But now I am. Don't worry. I would have taken lunch if I'd wanted to."

Angel gave her a look that said that she didn't believe her.

Maggie sighed. "Okay, okay. Things are so busy right now at the café that I just don't have time during the day to eat." She looked around the table. "But don't worry, I intend to make up for that now." The waitress came back to take Maggie and Angel's orders.

Sarah eyed Dahlia. "Now that everyone's here, are you going to tell us your big secret?"

Dahlia took a big breath. "You know how Garrett and I have been talking about having kids soon?"

Sarah's chest tightened unexpectedly.

Dahlia dragged out the suspense for as long as possible, then her face broke out in a huge smile. "We're pregnant!"

Gretchen and Charlotte cheered.

"That's great news!" Charlotte said.

"Congratulations," Sarah said, trying to fight against the waves of pain welling up inside of her. Her friend had just announced amazing news, so why was she feeling like this?

"I'm so happy for you, Dahlia," Angel said warmly. "When is the baby due?"

"The middle of June." Dahlia's face was glowing with happiness now. "We're really excited. Garrett's already taken out his baby name book that he uses for character names and is trying to find the best boy and girl names."

Gretchen laughed. "Sounds like him. Just make sure you

don't end up with some over-the-top name like they have in some of his romance novels."

"Don't worry," Dahlia said. "I get final approval."

Maggie hadn't said anything yet, but after everyone had congratulated Dahlia, she said, "I guess then this is a good time for my news." She turned to face Dahlia. "It sounds like our babies are going to be born around the same time."

Gretchen squealed. "Are you serious?"

Maggie nodded, and Gretchen threw her arms around her.

"Wow," Angel said. "I can't believe you didn't tell me." She slugged Maggie lightly on the arm.

"I didn't want to say anything until we were out of the first trimester. I didn't want to tell Alex he was getting a sibling and then have it not come true. But now, I can't wait to tell the world." Maggie's face lit up.

Sarah looked down at her lap and pretended to be fishing for something in her purse while congratulations echoed around the table. Tears slipped from the corners of her eyes and she surreptitiously wiped them away before anyone could see her. Of her group of friends, she was the only one who hadn't met their "Mr. Right."

Would it ever happen? She'd thought Patrick might have been that person, but he was happy now with someone else. Maura had been busy since her date with Patrick and Sarah hadn't had a chance to talk with her about him, but why wouldn't they have hit it off? She pressed her lips together. He was such a nice guy – everything she'd ever wanted in a man. If only she hadn't set him up with Maura.

"Are you okay?" Charlotte asked in a low whisper.

"I'm fine." Sarah forced a smile onto her face. "I had something in my eye."

"Okay." Charlotte shot her a dubious look but didn't press the issue.

Sarah glanced up at Dahlia and Maggie who were chatting animatedly across the table about baby stuff. She looked back down at her half-full plate of nachos, but her appetite had disappeared. The cheese had congealed, creating an unappetizing mess of chips and salsa. She pushed it away.

"I'm so happy for both of you," Sarah said. "I'd better get going though. I've got papers to grade."

"See you later," Dahlia said. The others murmured their goodbyes as well and Sarah left.

When she returned home, she sat in her living room staring at the samples on the coffee table that Patrick had left for her. He'd made an effort to bring her these and she'd thought maybe he had feelings for her, but his abrupt departure had proven otherwise.

---

13

*A*fter working at the bookstore all weekend and then getting some things ready in her classroom while the kids were on break, Sarah completely forgot about buying a Thanksgiving dinner for Tommy's family until Tuesday evening. She managed to find everything at the grocery store – except for a turkey. Every unfrozen turkey in Candle Beach was sold out, so she called the one person she knew who could always manage to magically pull things out of the air.

"Mom?" Sarah held the phone to her ear, crossing the fingers of her left hand. She needed any luck she could get to pull this off for Tommy.

"Hi honey," her mother said warmly. "How are you doing? Are you enjoying getting to have the classroom to yourself with the kids gone?"

Sarah laughed. "It has been nice. It's amazing how much faster things go without them there." She sobered. "But actually, I'm calling because I have a student whose family can't afford a turkey dinner this year."

"Oh," her mother murmured sympathetically. "Is there something I can do to help?"

"Actually there is." She looked over at the pile of food she'd bought from the grocery store. Without a turkey, it wouldn't be much of a Thanksgiving dinner. "I was hoping you might know of someone who has a defrosted turkey that I could give to them. The grocery store only has huge frozen ones left and they'll never thaw in time."

"Hmm. That is a tough order."

Sarah imagined her mother sitting in her favorite recliner in their living room, staring out the window.

"You know, I think I might know someone who has an extra. I'll check with them and call you back, okay?"

"Thanks Mom." Sarah hung up and got to work on the pumpkin pies she was baking, both for her own family's celebration and for Tommy's family.

A few hours later, her mother called back. "I've found you a turkey," she said triumphantly.

Sarah's spirits rose. "That's great."

"I'll have it for you by tomorrow morning, okay?"

"That's perfect. I'll stop by and grab it on the way over to my student's house with the other food."

They said goodbye to each other and Sarah hung up the phone. She eyed the line of pies that covered her kitchen table. Moving into a new house with more kitchen space would be wonderful. She got everything ready to take over to Tommy's house the next day and went to bed, feeling more optimistic than she had in a long time.

On Thanksgiving, Sarah went over to her parents' house early in the afternoon to join everyone for a turkey dinner.

She'd successfully dropped off the food at Tommy's house and his mother had shed a tear when she'd handed her the freshly baked pumpkin pies.

When she arrived at her parents' house, her older sister Jenny, along with her husband Rick and their two kids, was already there.

"Auntie Sarah!" five-year-old Kara shouted. "I'm so excited you're here."

As she allowed Kara to pull her down the hall to the room that Sarah's mother had outfitted with bunk beds and toys for the grandkids, she thought about how lucky she was to have her family. Even though she didn't have a special love interest in her life that year, at least she had them.

Later in the evening, when Adam and Angel were snuggled up together on the couch and she could hear Jenny and Rick joking with each other in the kitchen as they packed up leftovers to take home, she wasn't feeling so lucky. It seemed like everyone but her had someone special in their life. Kara seemed to notice how she felt.

"Auntie Sarah?" She tugged at Sarah's dress. "Do you want to come play dolls with me?"

Sarah looked around the living room again. Her parents were now talking with Angel and Adam, and she was acutely aware that she was the fifth wheel in the room.

"Sure honey. I'd love to." She and Kara went into the playroom and Kara handed her a Ken doll.

"They're getting married." She held up her Barbie doll, who was dressed in a long white gown.

"Oh." Sarah eyed them. Even with a five-year-old, she couldn't escape being around couples. She swallowed a lump in her throat. She'd hoped to have had a date lined up for Gretchen's wedding by now – maybe even Patrick – but that didn't look like it would be happening. It would be just one more event this holiday season where she'd have to fly solo.

She pasted a smile on her face and held Ken out in front of her. "Where should they get married?"

Kara grinned and pointed across the room at a tall dollhouse. Sarah felt a little better. At least her niece was happy.

The bookstore was closed for the evening on the Friday after Thanksgiving, but Dahlia knew Sarah was looking for extra shifts and had enlisted her to decorate the store for Christmas while it was free of customers. Charlotte had come downstairs to help her, and they'd turned it into an impromptu Christmas party, complete with sugar cookies and holiday music.

"Can you help me with this string of lights?" Sarah held out the end of a long string of multicolored lights.

Charlotte came closer and picked up the other end. "What are you doing with these?"

Sarah pointed at the front bay window where they usually had a seasonal display. "I'm going to put them around the inside of the window, so people can see them from the street and from inside the bookstore. Then I'll put some ceramic houses in the window and add some fake snow."

"Dahlia has ceramic houses?" Charlotte carried her end of the lights over to the window where there were already hooks above the window to hang them from. "I never pictured her as being that into Christmas."

Sarah laughed. "I have a bunch of ceramic Christmas village houses. I've been collecting them since I was a little kid. Dahlia thought it was a great idea to use them in the display, so I brought a few of them in."

"Good thinking." Charlotte watched as Sarah pulled the lights tight at the top. "Looks good."

Sarah plugged them in and the colorful lights flashed on, bathing the dark bay window in warmth. A sense of joy washed over her. There was something about the Christmas season that always made her happy, even when her personal life felt chaotic.

Charlotte followed Sarah to the bookstore's back room, where Sarah removed two medium-sized boxes from a larger box. They carried them to the bay window, and carefully unwrapped the tissue paper from around the contents.

"These are beautiful." Charlotte ran her fingertip along the faux snow coating the roof of a ceramic house.

"Thanks." Sarah laughed. "I know some people like to make fun of Christmas village displays, but there's something magical about them, as though you're getting to see the whole town from above, like it's set in a snow globe." She thought back to Patrick's expression when he saw her collection set up in her living room. Unlike most people, he almost seemed to understand how much decorating for Christmas meant to her. Her heart twinged, and she shook her head to remove any thought of Patrick. "Do you and Luke have any plans for Christmas?"

Charlotte shrugged. "I think we're going to be spending the holidays with our families in Haven Shores. My family always has very interesting holidays, and I'm not sure what Luke is going to think. They tend to go a little overboard with decorations and outdoing each other on gifts."

"Well, at least he's met them before and knows what to expect," Sarah said.

"Yeah, I guess. I'm looking forward to seeing Luke's

grandfather, Pops, on Christmas Eve though. We plan on having dinner with him and his friend at the retirement home."

"Will any of the rest of his family be there?" Sarah tucked the cord to one of the houses under a cloud of cottony snow.

"Luke doesn't have a very big family, but his sister is coming out to Haven Shores for the holidays. Actually, she's going to be staying with me since Luke's studio apartment is so tiny." Worry flickered over Charlotte's face.

Sensing her friend's concern, Sarah asked, "Have you met her before?"

"Kind of. I knew who she was back in high school because Luke and Parker were best friends, and Zoe is Luke's twin, but I haven't seen her as an adult. She's a wedding coordinator up in Willa Bay, so she doesn't get much vacation time to come visit." She twisted a red ribbon between her fingers. "I hope she likes me."

Sarah hugged her. "She'll love you. Don't worry."

Charlotte gave her a smile, but her lips wavered. "I hope so." She stood up straight and gave the display a discerning look. "I think it looks pretty good, at least from the back."

"Me too." Sarah flicked on the lights and gestured to the door. "Let's check it out from outside."

On the sidewalks outside, the street lights cast a warm glow but the air itself was cold and their breath came out in little puffs.

Sarah folded her arms across her chest. "Looks good." She knelt down. "Except that person in the corner. He's just standing there, looking like he has no idea why he's in the display."

Charlotte looked at the man and burst out in laughter.

"He looks as confused as I do when Luke starts telling me about software engineering."

They went back inside, and Sarah moved the figure over to stand near a woman who was watching children make a snowman. "There," she said. "Now he belongs." She stared at it wistfully.

"Are you okay?" Charlotte asked.

"I'm fine." Sarah turned away from the display.

"No, you're not." Charlotte's eyes narrowed. "Something's bugging you."

Sarah shook her head. "It's nothing. It's just hard seeing everyone so happy with their significant others. I thought maybe I'd have someone special to share the holidays with this year."

"Oh." Charlotte quieted for a moment. "I know all too well what that's like. Last year, I watched Dahlia, Gretchen, and Maggie fall in love and I spent Christmas wishing I'd finally meet the love of my life." Her face flushed, and she laughed. "Little did I know that I'd already met him." She peered at her friend. "Hey, do you want me to try to set you up with someone?"

Sarah shook her head vigorously. "Uh-uh. No blind dates. The last one I had turned out horribly."

Charlotte smiled and held up her hand. "Okay, okay. I won't fix you up with anyone." She appeared thoughtful. "I feel bad talking about Luke so much though. I hope it doesn't bother you."

"No, it's not that." Sarah sat down on the floor with her back against the wall. From there, she could see the entire bookstore. She stared at the window display they'd created. The image of the man and woman standing next to each other burned into her eyes. "The truth is, I can't get my friend Patrick out of my mind."

"Patrick?" Charlotte sat down across from her and eyed her critically. "Who's he? I don't remember you mentioning him before."

Sarah sighed. "I probably haven't, because we're just friends. He's a teacher I know. We met last year at the Drama in the Classroom course and I saw him again this previous summer." She flushed, remembering their kiss at the Fall Harvest Festival. "And a few other times since then."

Charlotte's eyebrows shot up. "You really like him."

"I do." Sarah's stomach lurched. "But he's dating someone else. My friend, in fact." She laughed ironically. "I even set them up."

"Ouch." Charlotte pushed herself up from the floor. "You know, this sounds like a longer discussion and we're getting too old to sit on the floor for long." She held out her hand to Sarah. "Want to raid Dahlia's coffee bar?"

Sarah laughed. Charlotte always knew what would cheer her up. "Coffee sounds perfect."

When they were settled on the stools at the coffee bar with steaming mugs of coffee in front of them, Charlotte's face turned serious. "So, this Patrick guy. What are you going to do about him?"

"What do you mean? I told you he's dating someone else." She shrugged. "There's nothing I can do about it."

"Have you told him how you feel?" Charlotte sipped her coffee, but Sarah could feel her eyes drilling into her face.

She squirmed. "No. Of course not."

"Well, you should," Charlotte said matter-of-factly. She set her mug down on the counter and uttered a long sigh. "Maybe he's secretly pining over you as well."

At that thought, a glimmer of hope rose up in Sarah's chest before she could tamp it down. She bit her lip and looked at Charlotte. "I sincerely doubt that."

"There's always a chance." Charlotte grinned. "I never thought Luke liked me before he asked me out. In fact, I thought he hated me."

Yeah, but he wasn't dating someone else, Sarah thought, but didn't say out loud. "Maybe."

"You should definitely say something."

Sarah's stomach tightened, and irrational annoyance flooded through her. She forced herself to be calm. Charlotte was happy in her relationship with Luke and she wanted the best for Sarah too. She knew that.

"I don't think this is the right time." She gulped her coffee, regretting doing so as the hot liquid burned her tongue.

"Maybe not, but when will it be?" Charlotte grinned.

Sarah couldn't take it anymore. "Can you please drop it?"

A wounded look came over Charlotte's face. "I'm sorry." Her eyes met Sarah's. "I just wanted to help."

Her stomach twisted. She knew Charlotte had been trying to help but it didn't matter if she told Patrick how she felt. "I know. But I don't really want to talk about it anymore, okay?" It was bad enough that she was alone for Christmas – she didn't need her friend constantly reminding her of that, or to face Patrick's rejection if she told him how she felt. Plus, she couldn't do that to Maura. She stood. "It's getting late. I'm going to turn off the lights in the window now, but I think Dahlia is going to love it when she comes in tomorrow morning."

Charlotte rose from her chair and hooked their coffee cups with her fingers, placing them carefully in the sink behind the bar. "I think she'll be pleased, especially to have decorating the store off of her plate."

After Sarah had the front of the shop closed up, she and

Charlotte walked to the back. Charlotte stood awkwardly by the staircase to her apartment above the bookstore.

"I really am sorry. I didn't mean to offend you about Patrick."

"I know." Sarah smiled at her. "Don't worry about it. I'll see you later, okay?"

"Goodnight." Charlotte's customary smile had returned, and she gave Sarah a little wave before walking up the stairs. Sarah went out into the back alley and locked the door behind her.

On the way home, she slowed her pace and took in the sights of Candle Beach as it prepared for Christmas. The town hadn't yet wrapped the lampposts in white and red ribbons, but they'd changed out the summer hanging flower baskets for heartier winter plants. This was her favorite time of year, so why wasn't she happier?

14

*A*lthough Sarah was a staunch supporter of the Haven Shores Children's Club, she'd been dreading their annual fundraising dinner for weeks. Everyone there, including some of her teacher friends, would attend with a date. Would Patrick be there? In case he brought Maura, she hadn't wanted to go alone, so she'd enlisted Adam to come with her. He hadn't been keen about dressing up for the event, but he'd reluctantly agreed to go with her. At least it wasn't a real date, so he wouldn't be forced to dance. That would probably have killed him.

A searing pain shot through her chest. Patrick would have been the ideal date but, of course, that wasn't an option. She'd considered Charlotte's advice to tell him how she felt, but it didn't feel like the right time to say anything to him. She hadn't seen or heard from him since he'd come to her apartment to bring over the samples. It was almost as though he was trying to cut himself out of her life completely. That was silly though. Maybe he was just caught up in the holiday rush like everyone else in the world.

She focused her attention on what mattered – getting

"Ma'am? Sir?" A waiter hovered near them, gesturing to a serving plate filled with flaky crab puffs.

Adam's eyes lit up at the sight of food. "Yes, thank you." He scooted several of the appetizers onto a napkin that the waiter offered him. Then he popped one of the bite-sized crab puffs in his mouth and chewed, a blissful expression coming over his face. When he finished swallowing, he said, "Now, this – this was worth getting dressed up for."

Sarah smirked. Her brother had never outgrown his childhood love of food, especially pastries. Still, she couldn't fault him. She'd swiped one off the tray too and it had been as flaky and delicious as it had looked. "I think they'll announce dinner soon."

"Ah." His eyes roved the large room. "I'll have to sample everything quickly then."

She groaned and shook her head but couldn't stop a smile from spreading across her lips as she watched him make a beeline for a uniformed waitress about twenty feet away. Then she caught sight of a man standing by himself in the corner of the room – Patrick. Although she wasn't surprised to see him because half of the teachers in the area were in attendance, she was surprised by the wistfulness that came over her. Even if they weren't meant to have a romantic relationship, she missed their friendship.

Should she go over to him? Was he here with a date? It had been a while since she'd spoken to Maura because they'd both been so busy with school, so she wasn't sure if they were still dating. She continued watching him, but he only sipped his drink and leaned against the wall. Eventually, a man in his forties approached Patrick and clapped him on the shoulder. They spoke for a while and she watched him unabashedly, until he suddenly turned and their eyes met. She quickly looked away. Had he seen her spying on him? If he hadn't had a reason to avoid her before, now he did. He probably thought she was some sort of stalker. She allowed herself a quick glance at him, but he hadn't moved.

When he finally parted ways with the other man, he started to walk in her direction, but then stopped.

"Look at all of these." Adam reappeared by her side with two small plates full of food and offered one to her. She reached for it automatically but didn't take her eyes off of Patrick. He'd turned completely around by now and appeared to be trying to get as far away from her as possible.

She sighed. "Thanks," she said as she accepted the plate. Might as well drown her sorrows in delicious food.

"Are you okay?" Adam popped the last bite of a jumbo shrimp into his mouth and stared at her.

"Yeah, I'm fine," she said sharply. His eyes widened, and she cringed at the hurt expression on his face. "Sorry, I don't mean to take it out on you."

"What's bothering you? Is it the stress of the new house?"

She looked at him. That was as good of an excuse as any since she didn't want to get into a conversation about her nonexistent relationship with Patrick. "Yeah, they haven't approved my loan yet because they keep losing my paper-work. It's starting to get to me."

He put his free arm around her waist and hugged her close to him. "Sorry, sis. I was a horrible mess when I bought the newspaper and my apartment above it. It's hard to spend your whole life savings on something and then just hope that it all turns out okay."

She allowed herself to lean into her big brother's arms, suddenly very aware of how anxious she actually was about the new house. "Thanks, Adam."

The light orchestral music stopped and a man at the front of the room cleared his throat before announcing into the microphone that dinner was about to be served. The cocktail portion of the evening had passed more quickly than she'd realized and half of the seats around the tables had already been claimed. At this rate, the evening would be over before she knew it.

"We'd better find a table," she said. Adam spotted two seats together at an almost full table and they nabbed them before they were taken. After introducing themselves to the rest of the table, who were all friends already, she found herself deep in conversation with the woman next to her about the state of education in the area.

Soon, dinner was served. While they ate, Sarah scanned the room surreptitiously for Patrick. She finally found him sitting at a table with several other people, but he didn't appear to have a date with him. Should she go over to him, or would that look weird? By the time she'd swallowed the last bite of her chicken cordon bleu, the decision had been made for her – the speeches had started.

After she fought to stay awake through an hour of dull speeches, a band set up on the stage broke out into a lively song designed to entice people out onto the dance floor. Sarah looked at Adam.

"Uh-uh." He shook his head. "Don't even think about it."

"Oh, fine." She loved to dance, but it wasn't in the cards for the evening. Besides, her feet were already killing her. She looked around the room, but Patrick had sneaked out while she'd been distracted by the band. Her mood deflated.

Why had he said nothing to her the whole evening? She knew he'd seen her, but he'd purposely snubbed her. Had their friendship meant so little to him? "We might as well head home now," she said.

"But what about dessert?" Adam hung his head like a puppy dog. "We can't leave before they serve dessert. I heard there's cherry cheesecake."

She had to smile. She knew he didn't want to be there, but he'd do anything for a dessert. "Fine, we can stay until after dessert."

By the time they got back to Candle Beach, it was after eleven o'clock and she was yawning – her normal bedtime was around ten because she liked to get to school early. Her feet were dragging as she walked up the stairs to her house.

She waved goodbye to Adam, who had waited in the car to make sure she got in safely. When she opened the door and stepped inside, he drove off. She closed the door firmly behind her, set her keys on the kitchen counter and kicked off her shoes as she walked toward the living room. They hit the wall with a dull clunk that echoed her mood. Even her cheery Christmas decorations failed to brighten her spirits. She'd never have thought her friendship with Patrick could dissolve so quickly. At least she had her new house to keep her mind off of him. Had the bank responded yet to the paperwork she'd sent them?

She sat down at her computer and clicked on her email. The bank she was using for the mortgage had sent her something. Her stomach filled with unease as soon as she skimmed the email from them. They needed more documentation about her pay – the same thing she'd sent them last week. She flipped the laptop lid down. She'd thought buying a house would be exciting, but, so far, it had been much more stressful than she'd anticipated. She leaned back in her desk chair, her feet aching from the shoes she'd been wearing. Tomorrow would be better. It certainly couldn't be worse.

15

The next day, Sarah couldn't take it anymore. She called Maura to find out if Patrick had said something to her about the charity dinner the night before.

"Patrick?" Maura asked.

"Yeah." Sarah paused. Why was Maura acting so perplexed? "He wouldn't talk to me at all. Do you know why?"

"No. Why would I?"

"Because you're dating him?"

Maura laughed. "We are definitely not dating. Why would you think that?"

"I don't know." Hadn't Patrick implied that he and Maura were dating? When she'd asked him about their date, he'd said it went well and then he'd changed the subject. She'd figured he felt awkward talking to her about it, but she'd obviously been wrong. "You seemed like you'd be perfect for each other and then neither of you told me how your date had gone, so I just assumed..."

"Well, we're not." Maura cleared her throat. "But it sounds like you could use someone to talk to. It's been a while since we hung out and I'm free today. Why don't you come over to my house for some tea or coffee? Would that work?"

Sarah surveyed her living room. It was a mess of boxes, both neatly packed and overflowing. There was still a lot to do before the closing on her new house – if that ever happened. But maybe getting away from it and seeing her friend would help the anxiety that rose up in her chest every time she thought about not getting the house.

"Sure. I'll be there in twenty minutes, okay?"

"See you then." Maura hung up.

Sarah grabbed her keys and her coat, then hiked over to Maura's house. The air outside was crisp and the sun bright. Usually the combination would lift her spirits, but today all the brightness did was numb her even more. She knocked on the door of Maura's cute blue house. Her friend hadn't gone all out decorating for Christmas yet, but she'd made a nod to the season with a fragrant wreath framing the knocker. The door swung open and Maura beckoned her in, leading her into a cozy kitchen.

"It was horrible, Maura." Sarah bent low over the cup of tea Maura had offered her. "He completely ignored me and acted like I wasn't even there."

"Maybe he didn't see you," Maura said helpfully.

"Oh, he saw me." She remembered the look on his face when he'd seen her there, like she'd stomped all over him or something, and then as suddenly as the expression had appeared on his face, it was gone, and so was he.

"So? Why are you upset about it?" Maura dunked a fresh tea bag into the steaming water she'd poured into her cup.

"Because we were friends. I even fixed him up with you and now look how he treats me." She sipped her too-hot tea.

Maura snorted. "You mean the date that didn't go so well?"

"Yeah." Sarah peered at her friend. "What happened with that? You didn't say anything to me afterward."

"Oh, I don't know," Maura said vaguely. "We just didn't hit it off I suppose. He seems like a great guy, but he's not *my* great guy. Besides, I get the feeling he has feelings for another girl."

"Oh." Sarah felt as though someone had punched her in the gut. "Well, she's a lucky girl. He's so nice and smart and handsome..." She trailed off, realizing she was babbling about someone she claimed was only a friend.

"Uh-huh." Maura stared at her. "If I didn't know better, I'd think you had feelings for him."

"No, of course not. He's only a friend." Her protest sounded flat, even to her, especially because her stomach still hurt from Maura's revelation. She fought for something to prove her claim. "Would I have set him up with you if I had feelings for him myself?"

"Maybe?" Maura put her teacup down on the table and took a bite of the miniature scones she'd removed from the oven after getting Sarah settled at the kitchen table.

"Well, I don't." Sarah bit into a scone so she wouldn't have to talk any more.

Maura peered at her. "Something's bothering you. If it's not Patrick, what is it?"

She swallowed, almost choking on the scone. The thought of Patrick dating someone else couldn't be bothering her, right? "Uh, yeah. It's this house thing. I still don't know if my loan will come through in time. I'm scared I'll lose the house to someone else."

"I'm sure it will be fine." Maura pushed the scone plate at her. "Have another. I think you could do with some carbs.

NICOLE ELLIS

Buying a house can be very stressful, but it will be so worth it in the end."

Sarah hoped Maura was right. At the moment, it was difficult to see the light at the end of the tunnel. She glanced around Maura's kitchen. Maura had an old-fashioned turquoise oven with four burners on top and she'd painted the rest of the kitchen a light blue, with a fleur-de-lis border at the top. The overall effect was enchanting, and she could see herself spending a lot of time in a kitchen like this. Maybe she should do the kitchen in her new house with a similar style. She found herself daydreaming for a minute about baking cookies in a beautifully renovated kitchen. Maybe she could talk her family into buying her things for her house for their Christmas gifts to her.

A realization hit her. Christmas gifts. She'd been able to buy and deliver some Thanksgiving fixings for the Jensen family, but would Tommy have any presents waiting for him under the tree?

"What's wrong?" Maura asked sharply, breaking into Sarah's thoughts.

"Oh, I was just thinking about one of my students. His dad was laid off from the mill last month and they're having some financial troubles." She frowned. "His parents are doing the best they can, but I don't think they'll have much money for gifts for the three kids."

Maura sighed. "It's so sad to see situations like that. Unfortunately, they're all too common here with the logging industry disappearing."

"I just wish there was something I could do." Sarah stared out the kitchen window.

"You could buy a gift for him and drop it off," Maura suggested.

"Yeah, but what about his siblings?" Inspiration struck.

"I bet I could get my friends to buy gifts for them, kind of like a giving tree."

Maura beamed. "That's a great idea. I'm in. Just let me know what to buy."

Sarah thought about it for a moment. "I'll come up with a list and then pass it around to my friends next time I see them." She felt as though a weight had been lifted from her chest. Unlike her friendship with Patrick or the house loan, giving Tommy and his siblings a merry Christmas was something she could influence.

The ringing phone woke Patrick from a nap on Sunday afternoon. He'd been up late the night before, working on the flooring in the upstairs bathroom, and he'd crashed after lunch. He fumbled for the phone, but only succeeded in knocking it to the floor where it bounced harmlessly off of the braided rag rug. When he finally managed to get ahold of the infernal device, he didn't recognize the number and considered not answering. Whether it was due to a sleep-addled brain or what, he didn't know, but he hit the green button to answer the call. Seconds later, he wished he'd let it go to voicemail.

"Are you playing some kind of game with Sarah?" a woman's angry voice blared over the line.

Patrick winced and held the phone away from his ear. "What? Who is this?" Unless she'd guessed the name Sarah, by some coincidence, she seemed to know him.

"It's Maura. Sarah Rigg's friend." She sighed dramatically. "Remember, you professed your love for another woman to me even before our first date was over?"

"Oh. Right. Hi, Maura." He threw the sheet off of his legs

and sat up in bed, rubbing his eyes to bring them into focus. "I still don't know what you're talking about though."

"Why are you ignoring Sarah?" She sounded even more exasperated this time.

"I'm not," he said automatically.

"Then why did she call me in tears this morning because you snubbed her at the Haven Shores Children's Club dinner?" Maura demanded.

A lead balloon slammed into him and he was instantly awake. "I didn't snub her. Or at least not on purpose. I saw her there with her date and I didn't want to bother her." At least that was what he'd told himself. In truth, it had hurt to see her there with the same man who'd come over to her house for dinner the day he'd brought the tile samples.

"C'mon, Patrick. You said you had feelings for her. How has it taken you this long to tell her?" Her voice grew louder and faster as she spoke.

"She has a boyfriend," he protested. "What's the point in telling her?" He had to admire Maura's dedication to her friend. She was yelling at someone over the phone that she barely knew, on behalf of a perceived slight against her friend.

"No, she doesn't." Maura sighed again, as if exasperated. "Why do you think she has a boyfriend?"

His mind spun rapidly, and he stood, pacing the floor in front of the bedroom window. "She was at the event last night with some man. And I saw him go into her apartment with flowers a month ago."

"Really," Maura said, her tone implying he was an idiot. "Did she say this man was her boyfriend, or did you just assume?"

"Uh…" She had him there. Had all of this been a big misunderstanding? He stared at the bare branches of the gnarled tree outside of his bedroom window. "So if the man with the red hair isn't her boyfriend, who is he?"

Her laugh echoed over the phone line. "Red hair? That's got to be her older brother Adam. He owns the newspaper in Candle Beach." She paused for a moment. "You know, she probably did invite him to the fundraiser last night. They're pretty close."

Her brother? He'd ruined any chance of dating Sarah because he'd mistakenly assumed that her brother was her boyfriend? It did make sense though – she hadn't tried to hurry him out of her apartment when he'd brought her the samples and she'd never mentioned seeing someone else. Ice filled his veins.

"She hates me now, doesn't she?" He paced the floor in his bedroom, the hardwood cold under his stockinged feet.

"Are you really that dense?" she said. "If she called me that upset because you didn't talk to her at the event, she obviously has feelings for you."

"Thanks." He didn't usually take to being called dense, but this time he deserved it. "Do you think she'd agree to see me?"

"I don't know," Maura said. "She's pretty mad right now. You might want to give her a bit of time to cool off."

"Did you tell her I have feelings for her?" He ran his fingers through his hair. This was becoming very middle-schoolish and he was starting to think he'd need to pass her a note via a friend like his students did.

"No. I promised you I wouldn't tell her, and I keep my promises." She cleared her throat. "Look, I've got to go, but I thought you should know how she feels. Do with the information what you wish."

"Thanks." The phone clicked off in his ear and he set it down on the bedside table. Sarah didn't have a boyfriend.

He'd spent the last month assuming she did and trying to stay away from her. And for what? He'd only managed to upset her and make things worse between the two of them. Should he go to her house? Would she even want to talk to him? He groaned. When did life become so complicated?

16

"What do you think about this for Kara for Christmas?" Sarah held up a pink shirt with a glittery unicorn on it. The fluorescent lights overhead hit the shirt, causing it to sparkle.

Adam raised his eyebrows and wrinkled his nose. "Does she like glitter?"

"What five-year-old girl doesn't like glitter?" Sarah turned the shirt back toward herself to take another look at it. Yep. Her niece would flip out when she unwrapped it on Christmas.

He shook his head. "If you say so. I was thinking about getting her a toy. Every kid should get toys for Christmas."

"Okay, but what are you going to get for Charlie?"

"Uh, a toy?"

Sarah laughed. "To the toy store."

She picked up the two paper bags full of presents she'd found already for her family. Every year since she'd been home, she and Adam had gone Christmas shopping together and made a whole day of it. This year, they'd planned to go to the new sushi restaurant just outside the mall in Haven Shores. Her stomach grumbled just thinking about delicious salmon rolls.

"Let's find something so we can get to lunch," she said.

"Good plan. That pretzel shop we passed is making me hungry." Adam quickened his pace in the direction of the toy store.

She grinned. When was Adam not hungry? She had to agree with him though. The aroma of freshly baked pretzels had made her even hungrier.

"What did you get Angel? Earrings? A necklace?" She walked double-time to keep up with him as he weaved his way through the crowd.

While she'd detoured into the body care products store to get the cherry almond lotion that their mom liked, Adam had disappeared into the jewelry store, so she hadn't yet seen what he'd picked out for his girlfriend. She was pretty sure he hadn't bought an engagement ring for Angel, although it wouldn't surprise her if he popped the question sometime soon. She'd never seen her brother so happy as he was since he started dating Angel last winter.

"I found a silver heart pendant necklace with small diamonds on it." He looked satisfied with himself as he paused in a corner of the toy store. "Want to see?"

"Of course." She waited while he pulled out a plastic bag emblazoned with the name of the jewelers on it from a much larger bag of presents.

He removed a small white clamshell box and showed her the necklace inside. "I hope it's okay." His hands shook as he handed her the box.

She sucked in her breath as she pried open the lid. The diamond-accented pendant was sparkly and beautiful, the adult woman's equivalent of a unicorn t-shirt. If someone gave her a gift like that, she'd never take it off. "She's going to love this."

A look of relief spread across his freckled face. "Oh, good. I never know what to buy women. But this one caught my eye and the lady in the store seemed to think it was nice."

"Well, you don't have to worry about this one. There's no way she won't like it." She handed it back to him and he carefully tucked it away in the bag. If only she had someone that cared about her as much as her brother obviously did for his girlfriend. She swallowed a lump in her throat. It was looking like she wasn't going to have a chance for love like that anytime soon.

Adam seemed to notice her expression and his gaze drilled into her. "Okay, what's going on with you?"

His concern was too much, and she couldn't stop a tear from slipping out of her left eye. She tried to surreptitiously wipe it away, but he caught her movement. Behind them, the cash register cha-chinged and the line to pay stretched halfway to the back of the store.

"Are you crying?" His face was panic-stricken. "Did I say something wrong?"

"No." She wiped away more wet tears as they slid down her cheeks. "You didn't do anything wrong. I'm probably just getting hungry and tired." Although everyone else in the toy store seemed focused on their gift lists, she was mortified to be practically bawling in the middle of the store.

He put his bags down and wrapped his arm around her shoulder. "I know you. This is more than hungry and tired. What's wrong? Did someone do something to you?"

She shook her head, fighting back tears. "No."

He somehow managed to pick up all of their bags full of gifts and guided her to a bench in a quieter, side area of the mall. She collapsed onto the hard wooden seat, grateful to be away from most of the shoppers.

"Thanks." She took a deep breath. "Sorry. I don't mean to ruin our shopping day."

"You're not ruining anything." He regarded her with concern. "But I don't think I've seen you cry like that since you were a little kid. Is it the house? Did the mortgage not go through?"

She shook her head. "No. When I called them yesterday, they finally had received everything and said it was good to go. I should be able to close on the house soon."

"Then what is it? Is there anything I can do about it?" He stared at her in wide-eyed panic.

She rummaged through her purse and pulled out a Kleenex to dry her eyes. "There isn't anything you can do about it. This is going to sound stupid, but it's about a man that I kind of had a crush on." Before he could say anything, she said, "I know, I know. It's childish. But Patrick's a great guy and I can't help it. Unfortunately, we're just not meant for each other."

"He can't be that great if he's not interested in you." He'd puffed up in the over-protective big brother way she'd seen when her high school romantic relationships hadn't worked out.

"He was dating someone else when we met. And then he wasn't. And he fixed me up with his friend, so I know he doesn't have feelings for me." She dabbed at her eyes. It all sounded so convoluted when she told him about her relationship with Patrick.

"But the blind date didn't work out?" Adam asked, as if trying to figure out the timeline of events.

"No. The guy he set me up with wasn't my type."

"And this guy, Patrick, he's your type?"

"Yes." She nodded miserably. "But if he set me up with his friend while he himself was single, he's not into me, right?"

Adam shrugged. "I can't answer that. I can tell you that we men, including myself, can't always express ourselves in the right way. Maybe he was scared that you wouldn't reciprocate his feelings, so he pushed you in the direction of his friend. Or maybe he just sees you as a friend. I don't know."

She slumped against the back of the bench. "So I'm stuck pining over him forever?"

He smiled at her. "Why don't you tell him how you feel and find out how he feels? That's the only way you're going to find out what he truly wants."

"I don't know. That sounds like a good way for me to get hurt." She stared out at all of the happy shoppers. A little kid walked by holding his mother's hand, pointing at items in the toy store window to add to his Santa wish list. The child's father walked up to them, winking at the mother and pointing first at the bag he held, then at the child. They shared a conspiratorial grin over the bag that probably held the child's Christmas gift.

Her stomach twisted. She wanted that kind of private moment and sense of companionship for herself. She wanted her own little family. And she wanted a chance to have that with Patrick. But to find out if there was any possibility of that for the two of them, she needed to put herself out there.

"You there?" Adam peered at her anxiously.

"Yeah." She lifted her head and met his gaze. "I think you're right though. If I don't tell him, I'll never know." How she was going to tell Patrick how she felt, she didn't know. But she couldn't continue to feel this miserable – it was ruining her favorite time of year.

"Good." He stood from the bench. Apparently, to him, the matter was settled. "Now, let's get back to toy shopping. There's a Nerf gun in there that I want to try out for Charlie."

"You just want to try it out for yourself," she teased. Making the decision to talk to Patrick had lifted a weight off of her chest and she now felt ready to have fun on their annual brother-sister Christmas shopping day.

"Maybe?" He laughed and grabbed her free hand, dragging her into the shop with him. She allowed him to pull her over to the Nerf gun section and soon found herself shooting foam bullets at a target the store had set up along the back wall. Her love life may be in a shambles, but at least she had her family. Spending the day with her brother had turned out to be exactly what she needed.

17

*M*aggie's event setup crew had outdone themselves decorating the Sorensen Farm for Gretchen and Parker's wedding. In the spirit of a winter wedding, red and white bows had been tied to the trees on the property. One of the larger trees had been decked out in multicolored lights with a star on top.

Sarah exited her car and shivered in her ankle-length green dress. The doors to the barn weren't too far away, but she threw on her wool peacoat anyway. Better to be safe than sorry in case she decided to go outside during the event. Adam and Angel had offered to drive with her to the wedding, but she'd opted to go by herself. Then she could leave whenever she wanted to and not have to wait for them.

"Sarah!" a woman cried out from behind her. She turned to see Charlotte running toward her in a red satin bridesmaid dress. Her hair was perfectly coiffed, and her face flushed.

Charlotte bounced up to her, grinning. "Isn't this exciting? I love weddings."

Sarah couldn't help but smile at her friend's enthusiasm.

"It looks like it'll be a beautiful wedding." She glanced up at the sky. "The weather forecaster said it might even snow tonight."

Charlotte looked up as well. "Wouldn't that be lovely? I bet they'd get some great pictures."

"Aren't you cold?" Sarah asked, hugging her coat to her chest.

Charlotte shrugged. "A little." She motioned to the farmhouse. "We're all getting ready in there. Do you want to come hang out with us?"

"Uh…" She looked at the house. "I'm not in the wedding party, do you think Gretchen would want me there? I don't want to make it overcrowded."

"Nonsense." Charlotte tugged at her hand. "C'mon."

Sarah followed her back to the house and into the warmth of the farmhouse's kitchen. She removed her jacket and Charlotte gestured for her to follow her down the hall to the room Maggie and Jake had left available for wedding parties as a bride's room.

When they entered, everyone was dressed and buzzing with excitement. Gretchen's other bridesmaids, Maggie and Dahlia, wore the same red gowns as Charlotte. Angel had a bobby pin in her mouth and was standing on a stool trying to artfully pin a curl to the side of Maggie's head.

"Hey, Sarah. I'm so happy you were able to make it." Gretchen tottered over to them in a floor-length satin gown with a train that trailed behind her.

Sarah leaned in to hug her. "You look gorgeous."

"Thank you," she said happily as she smoothed her hands over her dress. "I'm not usually one for wearing fancy clothes, but I love this dress." She checked her reflection in the mirror. "There's something about having beads on a dress that make it that much more special."

Sarah smiled. "I love the beading on the bodice." She pointed at Gretchen's feet. "And you have Cinderella shoes too."

Gretchen lifted up a foot to show off her faux clear glass slippers. "I know. I found these online and couldn't resist." She laughed. "If I'm going to look like a princess for the day, I might as well go all out."

Maggie tapped her watch. "Hey, girls. We've got to get finished up here. We're supposed to be on in twenty minutes."

"Oops, Maggie's right. I'd better finish up my makeup." Gretchen hugged Sarah again. "I'll see you at the reception."

"I'd better go find a seat," Sarah said.

"I'll come with you," Angel said. "Adam was supposed to save seats for us both, but I never know if he'll get to talking with someone and forget."

They exchanged knowing looks. Adam wasn't perfect, but he was a great brother and Sarah was happy to know that he'd found his perfect match in Angel. Before she'd come to town, Adam had been happy enough, but Angel brought something wonderful out in him, like he'd been waiting for her to come to Candle Beach to complete his life.

Tears sprang to her eyes – partly out of happiness for her brother but also because she didn't know if she'd ever find for herself what he and Angel had. For her, love always seemed just out of reach. She straightened her spine and resolved that the very next time she saw Patrick, she'd tell him how she felt. If he didn't reciprocate her feelings, so be it. At least she'd have tried.

Sarah waited as Angel gathered up her belongings and put on her high-heeled shoes.

"Okay," Angel said as she scanned the room. "I think I have everything. If not, it'll still be here after the ceremony."

They walked over to the barn together and walked inside, stopping near the entrance.

"I love these decorations," Angel said as they admired a large bouquet on the table with the guest book.

"Me too." Sarah lightly ran her finger over the velvety petals of a red rose. All of the floral arrangements were red and white roses mixed with feathery baby's breath. The result was pure winter elegance.

"Do you see Adam?" Angel craned her neck to see both sides of the aisle. "Ah! There he is. I see his hair."

Sarah chuckled. "I always tease him that his red hair glows."

Angel quickened her pace to reach Adam. He'd saved two seats next to him and Sarah watched as he reached for Angel's hand and guided her into the row next to him. Sarah was about to follow when she saw Patrick sitting a few rows back with an empty seat beside him. She hasn't expected to see him there, but he was a friend of Parker's.

The room froze, and all sound condensed to a dull hum in her ears. A myriad of conflicted thoughts danced through her mind. She'd promised herself that she'd tell him how she felt the very next time she saw him, but was this the appropriate place to have that conversation? She turned her attention back to Angel and Adam, snuggling against each other with their chairs pressed closely together. Safety, or a chance for a new future?

She squared her shoulders and forced herself to walk toward Patrick. Her shoes tapped along the hardwood floors of the barn, forming a rhythm that rocketed through her brain. Within moments, she was standing next to him. His attention was focused on the wedding program on his lap and he didn't see her.

Inhaling deeply, she tapped him on the shoulder. He looked up, his face registering surprise.

"Sarah."

She nodded dumbly, then pointed at the empty chair next to him. "Is this seat taken?"

"No," he said softly.

She nodded and brushed past him to get into the seat. Her bare legs grazed the crisp fabric of his suit pants, sending shivers up her spine. Her heart was beating so fast that she thought she'd soon pass out, but she managed to seat herself and straighten the skirt of her dress over her knees.

She glanced over at him. He was staring straight ahead, his lips pressed together. She couldn't help remembering how magical their kisses at the harvest festival had been. More than anything, she wanted a chance for a future with this man.

"Patrick…" she started to say. He turned to her, but the music started, and the barn doors slowly opened.

She went silent and everyone in the room watched as Maggie, Dahlia, and Charlotte came through the doorway, carrying small bouquets of red and white roses. They beamed at everyone as they walked by.

After they reached the front of the room, where a very nervous-looking Parker stood next to the minister, Gretchen's dog Reilly came trotting down the aisle wearing a pillow with the rings securely attached. Sarah smiled at the ecstatic look on the dog's face as he approached Parker.

Then, the Wedding March began. Everyone stood as Gretchen began her walk down the aisle, stepping slowly on the hardwood floors with her beaded white train trailing behind her. She carried a large bouquet of red roses, tied with a simple white sash.

Sarah was breathless, watching her friend make her way to the front of the room where the man she loved stood at the altar. She allowed herself a peek at Patrick. He stood there, watching the bride walk up the aisle. As Gretchen handed her bouquet to Maggie to hold while she said her vows, Patrick turned slightly to the left and smiled at Sarah – a smile that held a great deal of promise. Sarah's heart melted. The air was full of romance. Was she finally going to have her chance too?

Parker and Gretchen recited their vows, their eyes brimming with love for each other. When the minister pronounced them husband and wife, a loud cheer rose up from the audience. Maggie handed Gretchen back her bouquet and the newly married couple walked back down the aisle, together.

Sarah couldn't hold back any longer. "Patrick," she whispered as she placed her fingers lightly on his arm.

He turned to her. "Sarah." An unspoken connection formed between them and he reached for her hand, strengthening the feeling. He squeezed her hand, sending threads of anticipation racing through her body. His hand was warm and comforting in hers.

She looked forward and saw Adam and Angel staring at her from where they sat. When Patrick had his attention turned toward the back of the room at the departing couple, Adam pointed at him and mouthed Patrick's name.

Sarah nodded, and her brother gave her a thumbs-up. She blushed and turned away, but didn't release her grasp on Patrick's hand.

When they were released by rows, Sarah and Patrick put on their coats and left the barn, still holding hands. They walked in silence down to the shores of Bluebonnet Lake. He rubbed his thumb along the back of her hand, awakening the nerves in a delightful manner.

After they had attained a measure of privacy, he stopped, and they faced each other.

"Sarah – I need to tell you something."

"Me too," she uttered.

"I haven't been able to take my mind off of you since we saw each other last summer."

"Me neither." They were both quiet for a moment, getting lost in each other's eyes. Then she laughed, breaking the spell. "Why were we so ridiculous? If you had feelings for me, why didn't you say something?"

"I don't know." He sighed. "I wasn't sure you felt the same way. You never said anything to me."

"I thought you were engaged," she pointed out.

He looked sheepish. "Yeah, I didn't realize that until later. I just thought you weren't attracted to me."

"So that's why you fixed me up with Derek."

"And then it snowballed, and you played matchmaker between Maura and me."

"Yeah." She laughed at how silly it had all been. They'd wasted so much time that they could have spent together. "You convinced me to date your friend and you knew I was single, so I assumed you weren't attracted to me."

He ran his fingers through his hair. "It was completely the opposite of that. I didn't want to have you reject me, so I pushed you away first." He looked deeply into her eyes. "Do you think you can forgive me?"

She gazed up at him and wrapped her arms around his neck. "I think so."

He bent down and briefly kissed her, his lips softly meeting hers. It felt every bit as wonderful as when she'd kissed him at the harvest festival. The clean, crisp air enveloped them, and she yearned to press closer to him to keep warm.

As if reading her mind, he began brushing an errant strand of hair from her face with a tremulous hand, only to continue by running his fingertips through it toward the back of her head. She closed her eyes, drinking in the experience of his touch. Her scalp tingled pleasantly as his fingers ran their course, until with a light pressure just above her neck, they pulled her in. Their lips met again. Bracing her against the cold, a warmth born of desire spread from the pit of her stomach, across her chest, ultimately flushing her cheeks. Closer! She wanted to be closer still.

A hand pressed against her waist, before moving to her lower back to pull her into the tighter embrace she desired. She broke away briefly for air, then pressed her lips eagerly into his again. She ran the fingers of one hand through the bristly hair at the base of his neck while the other clung to the back of one of his shoulders tightly.

She felt she could stay in this moment for an eternity. But slowly, the sounds of bustling people a short distance away began to pull her out of the trance.

Above the lake, people were filing back into the barn.

"They must have the tables set up in there for dinner." Sarah pointed up the hill. "Do you want to go back now?"

He nodded. "Let's go." He reached for her hand, giving it a gentle squeeze as he took it, to walk together back to the barn.

The space had been reconfigured for an evening of dinner and dancing. The white wooden chairs that had once formed rows on either side of the aisle now surrounded round tables lining the side of the room.

They found a seat at a table with Angel and Adam, who wisely only smiled at them but said nothing. After a delicious dinner of filet mignon and salmon, the catering staff cleared their plates and the festivities began.

Charlotte climbed onto her chair to toast Gretchen and Parker, her brother. "To my new sister. Thank you for turning the jerk who stole my Barbie dolls as a kid into the man he is today." She laughed and tipped her glass at them. The newlyweds smiled.

Others gave their toasts and then the cake was cut. Gretchen couldn't resist smashing it into Parker's face and they both ended up laughing, with their faces covered in white frosting.

Sarah took a bite of the vanilla cake and her eyes widened. "There are strawberries in this. It's so good."

"I'm definitely going back for seconds," Adam said, halfway through a large slice. Beside him, Angel sighed, but a wide grin had slid across her lips. "This isn't his first slice of the day. I made the wedding cake and, today at lunch, he sampled a few pieces of the trial cake I made a few days ago."

Patrick looked at Sarah quizzically.

"My brother loves sweets. It's kind of the family joke."

"Ah," he said. "I hope to meet the rest of your family soon too." He turned to Angel. "You're a wonderful baker. This is the best wedding cake I've ever had."

Angel blushed and gave him a small smile. "Thanks."

Sarah's stomach flip-flopped at Patrick's mention of her family. He was serious about her if he wanted to meet them already. And that was fine with her. She'd never felt so strongly about any man in her past and had a sneaking suspicion that this was the man she was meant to be with.

"Time for the garter toss," Parker called out.

The women hooted and hollered as all of the unmarried men gathered around and Parker removed the garter from

Gretchen's leg. She winked saucily at the crowd and everyone laughed. Patrick reluctantly joined in and Parker slingshotted the garter straight to him.

He looked up in surprise to find Parker grinning at him.

"I caught the garter at Dahlia's wedding and now look where I'm at. Good luck, buddy." Parker winked at Patrick.

Everyone laughed, and Patrick glanced at Sarah. She laughed too and smiled at him to let him know she wasn't intimidated.

As the evening wound down, Sarah and Patrick were two of the last people out on the dance floor. He swung her around slowly, their feet tapping against the hardwood floors. She felt deliciously intoxicated, not by alcohol but by the feeling of being near him. He leaned down and kissed her, dipping her a bit as he did so. She felt weightless and dreamy at the same time.

Too soon, the evening came to an end, but she knew it wasn't the end for them. Their story was just beginning.

"I'll see you tomorrow?" Patrick asked as he rested his hand on her open car door.

Sarah sat in the driver's seat, gazing up at him like a love-struck teenager. "See you tomorrow." They'd made plans for dinner the next night and she couldn't wait to see him again.

He stooped to kiss her cheek, then shut the door and walked away, stopping once to look back at her and give her a smile that made her heart flutter. She started the engine and drove back to the main part of Candle Beach, still stunned by the night's events. Had that really happened? Had her dream really come true? If it had snowed, she would have been sure that she was lost in a perfect fantasy. She gave herself a pinch on the thigh as she drove to make sure. Yes. It had really happened. She and Patrick had finally told each other how they felt.

18

*S*arah looked around the kitchen of her rental house with satisfaction. Most of the shelves and drawers were empty now and she was on track to finish packing on Sunday in preparation for the movers coming the next weekend. Buying a house hadn't been easy, but she'd finally closed on the property a few days prior and she was ready to move. She'd even taken down all of her Christmas decorations and the walls were bare of pictures. It looked much like it had the day she'd moved in a few years ago. A pang of nostalgia hit her, and she sat down at the kitchen table, idly wrapping some china dishes as her gaze floated around the room.

Her life had been so different four years ago. She'd returned to Candle Beach to take a job at the elementary school and found that all of her friends from high school had left town. She still had her family around, but it had been a lonely few years – until she'd made new friends – and until she met Patrick.

A warmth spread through her. Patrick. It had seemed like the time would never be right for the two of them and it still amazed her that things had worked out. In the last week, they'd spent every day together after her shift at the bookstore. Between her full-time job as a teacher, the bookstore, Patrick, and getting ready for the big move, she'd never been so busy – or so happy.

From the entrance to her house came the plop of a letter being dropped through the mail slot in the front door and landing on the floor mat. She finished wrapping a teacup in old newspaper and pushed her way through the stacks of boxes lining the hallway to retrieve her mail.

The mail carrier had left her a small, almost square, red envelope with her name printed on it in neat black script. She flipped it over to see the back. A snowflake-shaped white sticker held the envelope flap down and bore Maggie's name and address. Sarah slid her finger under the sticker and opened the envelope to reveal a Christmas card with an elf on the front. A whiff of something gingery wafted from the card. She grinned.

Christmas cards were one of her favorite parts of the holidays – a chance to reconnect with friends that she hadn't seen in years. With some of them, the annual Christmas letter was the only contact they had with each other and she cherished the news of old friends and their families. The wide mantel above the fireplace in her new house would be perfect for displaying the cards.

However, instead of a regular Christmas card this was an invitation to a Christmas tea at Maggie's old farmhouse on the Sorensen Farm. A few months ago, Maggie had mentioned the possibility of hosting a small Christmas party for her friends at her house, but after she'd announced her pregnancy, Sarah wasn't sure she'd still want to do so. She returned to the kitchen and set the card down on the table she'd just vacated before grabbing the last stack of plates out of the cupboard. Having her group of girl-friends and Patrick in her life had made all the difference. Maura had even mentioned recently how happy Sarah seemed now.

She stopped and eyed the invitation. Her own life may have changed, but Maura didn't have many friends or any family in town to celebrate the holidays with. Why hadn't she thought about that before? She'd been so wrapped up in her own life lately that she'd never stopped to think about her friend.

Where was her cell phone? She pulled a few boxes aside, lifted a pile of clothes she planned on donating to the Goodwill, then finally located it under a stack of newspapers she'd set on the coffee table. She called Maggie, who answered on the first ring.

"Hey," Maggie said warmly. "Did you get the invitation? Gretchen said she received hers today."

"I did, and I'd love to come. It sounds like so much fun." Sarah paused. She hadn't been friends with Maggie and the others until her brother had met Angel and she'd started working at the bookstore. Was it too much to ask for an invite for a friend? "Um, I was wondering if I could bring someone with me?"

Maggie hesitated, and Sarah held her breath. "Who did you have in mind?"

"One of my friends from work, Maura. She doesn't know many people in town and I thought it would be nice to introduce her to all of you. She could use some friends." She added hurriedly, "But if there isn't enough room for me to bring her, that's okay too."

Maggie laughed. "No, that's fine. We'd love to meet her."

"Thanks, Maggie." Sarah breathed deeply. "I'll see you in two weeks."

"See you." Maggie hung up and Sarah set her phone back down on the coffee table.

She looked around the room. There was still so much to pack before her move. Time to get back to work.

∾

The back door of the moving truck rattled as Patrick rolled it down to a closed position. He locked it and walked over to Sarah's new house.

"Is that everything?" Sarah asked as she came out of the house to stand on the lawn. Her face was flushed prettily and tendrils of her hair had escaped her ponytail.

He smiled. "Yep. That's everything."

A look of relief crossed her face. "Thank goodness. I never want to move another box again."

"Uh," Gretchen said, coming up behind her. "I hate to tell you, but every room of your house is filled with boxes."

"Okay, okay. I mean I never want to move houses ever again." Sarah glanced back at her house and beamed. "I'm here to stay."

"Good," Parker said as he wrapped his arms around Gretchen. "Because I don't want to have to help you move again. How'd you get so much stuff into that little house you were renting anyway?"

Gretchen glared at him and slugged him in the arm. "Never comment on how much stuff a lady owns."

He pulled his wife close to him and kissed her.

Patrick moved closer to Sarah and put his arm around her waist. "I'll call Pete's Pizza and order the food now."

She stood on her tiptoes to kiss him and his blood warmed. How was he so lucky to have her in his life?

"Sounds good. Thanks."

After the pizzas arrived, the four of them sat around the small table in Sarah's kitchen to eat.

"You're going to need a bigger table if you want to have all of us over." Gretchen glanced at the empty dining room. "I bet Garrett's mom, Wendy, has something gorgeous that she's refurbished. I think the dining room definitely needs a vintage piece."

"I agree." Sarah eyed the built-in china cabinet, just visible in the dining room through the open doorway from the kitchen. "I can't wait until I can hold parties of my own here."

Patrick loved the way her face lit up as she spoke, seemingly imagining parties in her new house.

"So, I don't know if this is an appropriate time," Parker said, turning to Patrick. "But have you given any thought to selling your house to my clients? After you let me show them the house, they fell in love with it even more, so they're willing to wait, but they need to move on if you're not going to be selling it."

Patrick looked at Sarah, took a deep breath, then smiled. She was his future, not some house filled with memories of Nina. "Yes. I'm ready to sell the house. I think if I hurry, I should be able to finish it up over Christmas break."

"Fantastic," Parker said. "They're going to be ecstatic to hear that." He turned to Gretchen. "Ha! I got this one."

She shook her head and smiled, then patted his hand. "Yes, you got this one. But I've still got you beat on sales for the year."

"Oh fine," Parker grumbled and took a huge bite of pizza, cheese dripping down his chin.

Patrick tried to hide his grin behind his beer bottle. The two newlyweds were cute together, something he hadn't anticipated ever thinking after Nina left him. Having Sarah in his life had given him a renewed faith in love. Although they'd only been together for a couple of weeks, he couldn't imagine a life without her.

"Speaking of real estate sales, we've got clients coming into the office this afternoon." Gretchen stared ruefully at the sweatshirt with holes in it and tattered jeans that she'd worn for helping Sarah move. "We'd better go home and get changed before we meet with them or they'll think we're not very professional."

Parker checked his watch and grimaced. "Where did the time go?" He stood from the table. "Thanks for the pizza, guys. This was fun and I hope to be invited when you have that big party you're dreaming of."

"You and Gretchen will be first on the list," Sarah said. "And any thanks should go to the two of you. I couldn't have done this without your help." She and Patrick walked Parker and Gretchen to the door.

After their friends left, Patrick turned to her. "Are you going to start unpacking?" He hoped she'd say no because his legs were killing him from both loading and unloading the moving truck, but if she insisted, he'd be happy to help.

Sarah scrunched up her face. "I know I should, but I can't convince myself to start." A mischievous gleam came into her eyes. "What would you say to playing hooky? We could set up the TV and DVD player and watch a movie. At least I can find the couch."

Thank goodness. He laughed. The floor was covered in boxes and even the couch was buried under some smaller items, but she'd labeled the boxes well. It shouldn't take much time to locate the DVD player. "I'll find the DVD player and the movies."

Later, when they were sitting together on the couch, he studied Sarah's face as she watched one of the twenty-odd

Christmas movies he'd found in a box. Happiness filled her face and he put his arm around her, relishing the feeling of being close to her. He wished every day could be like this one. But how realistic was that? He lived in a town thirty minutes away, which wasn't an insurmountable distance, but with both of them having full-time teaching jobs and second jobs as well, how likely was it that they could spend more than a day a week with each other?

He wasn't going to dwell on that though. They'd cross that bridge when they came to it. For now, he wanted to enjoy being with Sarah in her new house.

She sighed at a romantic part of the movie and snuggled closer to him. He leaned over and kissed the top of her head. She looked up at him and he bent down to kiss her.

"I could get used to this," she whispered before turning back to the movie.

He kissed her head again, her hair silky against his lips. "Me too."

CHAPTER 19 AND AUTHOR'S NOTE

A week later, a knock sounded on the door of Sarah's new house. She grabbed her winter coat from the hooks she'd hung by the door, and swung it over her shoulders as she pulled the door open.

"Hey," she said to Maura.

"Hey yourself." Maura peeked around her. "Do we have time for a quick tour of your new house? I haven't seen it yet, but the outside is really cute."

Sarah glanced at her watch. "Sure. We've got a few extra minutes."

She showed Maura around the house, her chest puffing up as Maura oohed and aahed over the built-in cabinets and the big backyard.

"You got a good deal on this place," Maura said as they walked down the front walk to her car. "I love it."

"Me too." A warmth spread through Sarah's body. Things were really starting to look up for her. A month ago, she hadn't been sure if the house purchase would go through and the idea of having Patrick in her life had been only a dream. She got into the passenger seat of

Maura's car and rubbed her hands together for warmth. "Brr."

Maura laughed. "I know. We live so close that my car was only starting to heat up when I pulled up to your house. But the heater should kick on soon." She started the engine, and true to her word, the heat came on immediately. She turned to Sarah. "So where is this tea party at? I know you said it was at a farm outside of town, but I've never been there before."

Sarah nodded. "The Sorensen Farm. Maggie and her husband Jake have turned it into an event center, but they live in an old farmhouse on the property."

"Ah." Maura navigated away from the curb. "So it's north of town?" She squinted against the bright sunlight streaming through the windshield.

"No, actually, it's south of town, right where the highway curves around Bluebonnet Lake." Sarah glanced out the window as Maura drove toward the main highway. Kids were playing in the park next to Main Street, taking advantage of the nice, sunny weekend weather. Sometimes it seemed like it had only been a couple of years since she'd swung on those same swings on a chilly day, her hands freezing to the metal chains as she pumped her legs to go higher. How had it already been decades?

She stared at the kids. Would her own kids be doing the same in a few years? She flushed. She and Patrick had only been dating for a few weeks, but somehow the idea of them having kids together felt right.

When they arrived at the Sorensen Farm, there were several other cars parked in the muddy parking area outside of the farmhouse. Maura parked next to a blue sedan that Sarah recognized from her house-hunting expedition as Gretchen's car.

Maura put her hand on the inside door handle but paused before opening it. "Are you sure it's okay for me to be here?"

"Of course." Sarah flashed her a quick smile. Maura wasn't usually this self-conscious, but this was a large group of people she'd be meeting for the first time.

Before they went inside, Maura opened the trunk and plucked out a bottle of nonalcoholic mulled cider and a bottle of glogg.

"You didn't have to bring anything." Sarah took the bottles from Maura as she shut the trunk.

"I know, but it makes me feel better." She took the bottles back from Sarah and they walked up to the wide front porch. The cheery yellow farmhouse never failed to make Sarah happy. It had been dark when she attended Gretchen's wedding, but in the light of day, she could tell Maggie and Jake had been busy. A garden had been created next to the house, with neat rows ready for next spring's planting. The corners of a new swing set in the backyard were visible over the fence line.

A dog barked excitedly behind the front door. Maggie opened it with a wide smile, while trying to keep the small white dog from escaping. "Sorry about Sugar. She's just happy to have so many new friends here today. You'd better come in before she gets out though."

They entered the house and Sarah leaned down to stroke the soft fur between the dog's ears. "She's beautiful. Did you just get her? I don't remember seeing her before."

Maggie grinned. "We've had her for a few months but kept her hidden away during Gretchen and Parker's wedding because Reilly was here. Besides, she tends to get overly excited around groups of people. Alex is in love with her." She half whispered, "Jake too, although he grumbles about her." She turned to Maura. "You must be Maura."

"I am." Maura handed her the bottles. "I thought these would come in handy."

Maggie read the label on the mulled cider. "Thank you so much. I'm sure they will. I haven't had this in a while, but I remember really liking it and I know the others will enjoy the glogg." She beamed at Maura. "Thank you. I'm so glad you were able to come." She gestured to some hooks on the wall. "You girls can take your jackets off here. The others are in the family room."

Sarah nodded, and they removed their jackets while Maggie disappeared in the direction of the kitchen with the drinks. Charlotte's laughter echoed down the hallway as they moved toward the family room.

"It sounds like they're having fun," Maura said, with a touch of hesitation in her voice.

"I'm sure we'll all have fun," Sarah said firmly. In a softer tone, she said, "Seriously, don't worry. My friends are great and will be happy to meet you."

When they turned the corner at the end of the hall, the space opened up to reveal two large couches surrounding a massive rough-hewn wood coffee table. A noble fir, decked out in brightly colored lights and a hodgepodge of fancy glass and children's decorations, dominated the room.

"Wow," Maura whispered. "That's one of the biggest indoor Christmas trees I've ever seen."

Sarah nodded. "Me too."

The other guests noticed them, and Charlotte jumped up to give Sarah a hug. "Hey. It's good to see you. Every time I see you nowadays, you're busy at the store and I don't want to bother you."

"I know. It's been crazy there." Sarah hugged her back.

"Crazy good business, you mean." Dahlia stood, her long gray sweater falling open to reveal a small baby bump. "This is the best holiday season we've had since I took over the bookstore." She eyed Maura with a question in her eyes.

Sarah realized she hadn't yet introduced her friend. "This is my friend Maura. She's a counselor at my school."

"Ah." Dahlia held out her hand. "Well, it's nice to meet you."

Angel, Gretchen, and Charlotte stood too to shake hands with Maura.

After the barrage of introductions, Maura laughed. "I hope I can remember everyone's names, but bear with me."

"Is everyone ready for some Christmas drinks?" Maggie asked from the hallway. "I've got coffee, tea, fruit punch, and Maura brought some glogg and cider too. There's something for everyone."

"Finally." Charlotte sighed dramatically. "I thought you'd never offer."

Maggie rolled her eyes. "You've been here all of ten minutes. You'll survive."

They followed her into the kitchen and then returned to the family room with their drinks.

"Where are Jake and Alex?" Sarah asked as she sipped her coffee.

"They went to a movie in Haven Shores." Maggie clutched her mug of chamomile tea. "Some superhero movie just came out that they were both dying to see." She rubbed her belly. "I'm glad they're getting along so well, but I'm secretly hoping this little one is a girl and will want to do things with me that I enjoy."

"I'm sure that whether the baby is a boy or girl, they'll want to do things with you." Gretchen smiled. "And hopefully with Aunt Gretchen too. I've got to live vicariously through you for a while because Parker and I aren't having kids for a few more years." She glanced at her tea dubiously. "In fact, maybe I shouldn't even be drinking the water – I think there must be something in it if you all are turning up pregnant."

Maggie laughed. "This baby was very planned. We didn't want to wait any longer because Alex is getting older." She turned to the others. "I've got a few games we could play if you'd like. Bunco is always fun."

"Sure," Charlotte said. "I love playing Bunco because you don't have to think too much and can focus on chatting and munching on goodies instead." She held up a plate full of cookies.

Sarah looked around the room. Now seemed as good of a time as any to ask if her friends would be willing to help with toys for the Jensen family. She cleared her throat. "Actually, before we start, I wanted to talk to you all about something." She explained the family's situation and pulled a list out of her pocket. "If we all choose one of the kids or the parents, they'd each get a couple of gifts apiece."

"I think that sounds like a great idea," Gretchen said.

Dahlia grabbed the list from Sarah and scanned it. "I can put together a package of books for the mom and dad. I bet they'd like that."

They divvied up the list and after fighting over who got to buy presents for the kids, they each took two names to buy gifts. Watching her friends argue amongst themselves to buy gifts for people they didn't even know made tears pool in Sarah's eyes. This was why she'd returned to Candle Beach – the community was always there when one of their own was in need. The Jensen kids would get a merry Christmas after all.

~

"Did she get them all?" Sarah peeked out from the other side of her car at the Jensen house. After they rang the doorbell, she and Patrick had scurried off of the porch to hide before anyone saw who had dropped off the mound of gifts on Christmas Eve. As they'd positioned themselves behind the car, Mrs. Jensen came out to see who was there. They'd watched as she picked up a gift, read the tag, then put a hand over her eyes to survey the neighborhood. Apparently not seeing them, she'd picked up an armful of gifts and carried them inside.

Patrick popped his head up over the trunk to look. "I think she got them all." He brushed some dirt off his knees.

"I hope Tommy likes the remote-controlled truck." She'd selected her student from the gift list. She shivered in the cold and blew on her hands to warm them. The temperature had dropped after dinnertime and it was now hovering around freezing. It wouldn't surprise her if it started snowing soon.

He put his arm around her. "I'm sure he'll love it. And the rest of the family will love everything your friends got them. I still can't believe you pulled this off with so little notice." He helped her up from her crouched position.

She shrugged. "My friends like to help." She slugged him lightly on the shoulder. "I saw you grabbed one of the names too."

His face flushed. "Pops and I had so much fun playing t-ball when I was a kid. I thought Tommy's little brother might enjoy it too."

They got into the car and took one last look at the house. Through the open curtains in the living room window, Sarah saw the family opening the Christmas gifts she and

Patrick had brought for them. A warmth spread through her when she saw the excited expression on Tommy's face as he pulled the truck out of the shiny blue wrapping paper she'd used.

"I told you." Patrick reached over and squeezed her hand, then maneuvered the car away from the curb and drove back to her new house.

When they arrived, he walked over to the other side of the car and opened the passenger door, offering her his hand as she stepped out. They walked up the concrete walkway hand-in-hand. She paused in front of the living room window to admire her collection of ceramic houses. They fit perfectly in the space, although there would be room next year for the ones she'd lent Dahlia for the book-store and any new ones she acquired.

When she opened the door, the aroma of freshly baked cookies hit them, even though they'd been removed from the oven a few hours earlier. They hung their coats by the front door and entered the living room.

"I'll grab us a plate of cookies and some coffee, okay?" she asked over her shoulder as she walked toward the kitchen. The counter was lined with white linen dish towels, covered with cheerfully decorated cookies. Most of them she'd take with her when she and Patrick attended her family's Christmas celebration the next day, but she'd made enough for home too.

"Sounds good."

When she came back into the room holding a cheerful, ornament-shaped red platter filled with several kinds of Christmas cookies, she found him staring at the fireplace mantel. He ran his hand over the solid wood.

"This is beautiful craftsmanship."

She nodded. "Every day, I find more to love about this house."

He looked at her thoughtfully. "You know, I was thinking."

She set the tray down on the coffee table in front of the fireplace. "Yeah?"

"How would you feel if I moved up to Candle Beach?" His gaze met hers. "I'm going to be selling my house to Parker's clients, and he's also asked me to partner with him on a home renovation business. I'd planned to buy another place in Haven Shores, but then I went house-hunting with you. I hadn't realized how many beautiful old homes Candle Beach has. I'm sure I could find a project up here. That way you wouldn't have to drive so far to visit me."

She felt his eyes on her face. How did she feel about that? She smiled at him. "That would be wonderful." She walked over to him and reached her hand up to his neck, pulling his head down to kiss him lightly on the lips. He grinned and surprised her by reaching for her waist and stepping sideways to the beat of Bing Crosby singing about a white Christmas. She allowed herself to lean into him and sway with him as he led her around the room in a slow, small circle.

As they moved, the colorful Christmas lights twinkled on the tree and in the window frame, casting a cheery glow throughout the room. He moved a hand off her waist to brush her hair away from her face and their eyes locked. He leaned down to kiss her, and the room seemed to melt away for a moment, as if they were standing in their own snow globe, cut off from the rest of the world. She tightened her grip around his neck and closed her eyes, enjoying the sensation.

He stopped moving and she opened her eyes. He turned her toward the window. "Look."

Outside, small flakes of snow were floating down from the sky, landing on the frozen sidewalk and blanketing it in white. She laughed. "A white Christmas."

He wrapped his arms around her as they stood there in the warm, cozy living room of her new house. "Just for you." He kissed the top of her head and she leaned against him, covering his arms with hers. As she looked outside, she imagined two little kids building a snowman together as she and Patrick helped them with the carrot nose and black button eyes.

She held onto him tighter, never wanting to let the feeling go. This was the beginning of all she'd ever wanted, and she knew that he was the man she wanted to spend the rest of her life with. As though he saw the same thing too, he squeezed her hands and then moved in front of her, gazing deeply into her eyes.

"I almost can't believe this is real. I've wanted it for so long." He smiled, tears pooling in his eyes. "With all the mishaps along the way, we truly must be meant to be together." He kissed her lips, then searched her face. "I love you."

With every muscle in her body feeling as though it had been turned to jelly, she leaned into him and met his gaze. "I love you too."

He pulled her close to his chest and they stood there together as the lights twinkled around them and the Christmas music continued to play.

Now this, is a perfect Christmas. Sarah melted into him, not thinking about anything other than how wonderful it felt to be there with Patrick.

Author's Note

I hope you enjoyed Sarah's story. If you did, please leave a review. I would really appreciate it! Reviews are a huge factor in a book's success and I'd love to write more in this series.

Thank You,

Nicole

Candle Beach Sweet Romances

Dahlia's Story (Book 1): Sweet Beginnings
Gretchen's Story (Book 2): Sweet Success
Maggie's Story (Book 3): Sweet Promises
Angel's Story (Book 4): Sweet Memories
Charlotte's Story (Book 5): Sweet History
Sarah's Story (Book 6): Sweet Matchmaking

Jill Andrews Cozy Mysteries

Brownie Points for Murder (Book 1)
Death to the Highest Bidder (Book 2)
A Deadly Pair O'Docks (Book 3)
Stuck with S'More Death (Book 4)
Murderous Mummy Wars (Book 5)
A Killer Christmas Party (Book 6)

<<<<>>>>